BLACK BUTTERFLY

BLACK BUTTERFLY

CLAUDIA JONES

Black Butterfly Productions, LLC
Signal Mountain, TN
2026

This book is a work of fiction. All the characters, organizations, and incidents are products of the author's imagination or are used fictitiously.

Published Independently by BLACK BUTTERFLY PRODUCTIONS, LLC
Address inquiries to author@claudia-jones.com
Printed in the United States of America

www.claudia-jones.com

BLACK BUTTERFLY © 2026 by Claudia Jones. All rights reserved. The reproduction or utilization of this work in whole or in part in any manner whatsoever is prohibited without the advance written permission of the publisher.

Book design by Tamian Wood, www.BeyondDesignBooks.com
Paperback: 979-8-9939669-0-8
Hardcopy: 979-8-9939669-2-2
Ebook: 979-8-9939669-1-5
Audiobook: 979-8-9939669-3-9

First Edition: 2026

DEDICATION

To my girls, and specifically to my tsunami; your force pushed me to break barriers that I would have never known to break without you.

PROLOGUE:

Perhaps we smell what we can't consciously fathom—a scent undetected. The attraction of the scent leads us to what we truly long for. It's an unconscious intelligence—almost instinctual.

What is there that we cannot see yet can perceive through our senses? Is there a sixth sense? A missing one? Or are there more things our senses notice that aren't consciously detected by the mind? Too much information in too little time; the brain can't keep up. Remember, the mind is not one of the senses—it's the vessel, the engine. Yet I find that the mind gets in the way of my senses. Can our thoughts and judgments hinder us from obtaining what we truly want, lead us astray? Maybe the whole somehow disrupts its parts.

My mind has led me astray, and I don't know how to get back. Yet within the mess of it all, I hear a rhythm.

LAKE LURE

The moment I walk into the cabin, the feeling of a fresh start rushes over me. The rental is fully delivering on its clichéd pitch: "Come to our cabin on Lake Lure and wash away your troubles." From the entrance, I notice a nice flow to the floorplan, even better in person than the pictures I received. The home is older, originally built in the 1940s. Subtle whiffs of wisdom echo throughout, yearning for recognition, as if it has a story to tell.

I walk farther in, and the door slams behind me. *It's just a gust of wind.* As I turn to the right and see the lake, my fear dissolves. The water is an alluring distraction. I'm drawn to it and move closer, like a force is pulling me.

Windows dominate the back of the house and provide a hundred-and-eighty-degree view. Looking out over the lake gives me the illusion that I'm in a ship. If I were a child, I'd spend hours imagining that I was the captain and planning where it would take me. The lake wouldn't be bound by mountains, but hidden crevasses in the coves would act as portals to other worlds or dimensions, or perhaps deliver me to another country.

Glistening in the sunlight, a glow emanates from it. The bordering trees are covered in bright spring leaves. The weather feels new, a perfect day. The mountains stage the backdrop with contrasting majesty.

The house rests in a lively cove, with people swimming, diving off docks, and kayaking. A teenage girl splashes a boy, and they tackle each other, crashing into the water's surface. Waterfowl bob with the wind current, dunking their heads underwater, tail feathers flipped vertical. It's a screenshot of a moment that could be painted and displayed right above my living room couch.

A smile crosses my face, and an overwhelming feeling of elation charges through my body. I want to join in and fully participate in this spectacle.

The lake continues luring me in, and I walk out onto the porch. I'm tempted to dive off the edge into the water because I know I can fly. If I jump, I'll land in a way that my body can handle, and the surroundings will support me.

I'm about to let the lake swallow me, or perhaps I'll glide over it, when there's a slight change in the sky. A cloud casts its shadow over the cove, and the lighting changes. It dims drastically and gets too dark too fast. Something is off. I stop and smell the air; it's no longer crisp, but stagnant.

I hear something beside me and realize that I'm not alone. I feel every follicle of hair stand up along my spine, from my tailbone to my neck. I turn my head and see her long, jet-black hair, the thickness covering her profile. I know her.

Her breathing is heavy and rapid. If I see her face, this will all be ruined. My happiness will disappear, my past will be resurrected. I turn further toward her and look past her long black strands. My eye is caught by one of my paintings in the corner of the porch, a childlike depiction of a boxed black butterfly. But she is there, so my attention returns to her.

I perceive her crazed smile and nervous energy. Trying my best to pay no mind to her, I turn back to look at the lake, and it's gone. Just a wall, no windows. I'm enclosed by black walls with no way out.

I wake up to my cell phone blaring its old-fashioned ringtone in my ear from my bedside table. I slap at it with one hand, and it falls to the floor. I bend down to see where it landed. The other side of the table. Trying to avoid getting out of bed, I stretch my arm as far as I can. The phone's still ringing, and I almost fall before my fingers finally wrap around it. I fling my head back to my pillow and collapse into the bed, my body a dead weight.

It's Chastain, my childhood friend. Exhausted, I hit Accept. "Hey, Chas...how are you?"

"Em, you sound tired. Did I wake you?"

I try to clear my head. "Yes...um...I was having a nightmare, so I'm glad you called."

"Reeaally?" Chastain must have already had her overdose of coffee for the day. "Do you want to wake up first or tell me about this chilling nightmare now?" The excitement in her voice makes it sound like she's ready to dish out some good gossip.

I sit up so I can respond with more energy. "No, I need to get up... It was just about... The cabin Arin rented for me; it felt like I was already there. I mean, the spitting image of the pictures. It was pretty, then it got dark, and then there was a person there."

"Umm...who was the person? An ax murderer? A possessed child?" Chastain asks, half serious, half joking.

Thank God for Chastain's overactive imagination. I dodge the question. "Ha, ha, Chas, no."

"Girl, if I were you, I'd cancel those plans in a heartbeat. It's a sign. Don't go."

"No, I need this trip."

"Right. You need it more than anyone I know, but that doesn't mean you should go to a strange town in the middle of nowhere by yourself."

"I like being alone; it inspires me. Besides, it was just a dream." I'm annoyed. Conversation before proper caffeine can go south quickly.

"Listen, my whole reason for calling is to have you send me the address and remind you to stay in touch while you're there so I'm not thinking you've been gobbled up by a bear or tortured by some lone woodsman or psychopath who locks you up in a basement and feeds you rat guts."

A quick laugh escapes. "Will you stop, Chas? Now I have a clear picture of a boogeyman to worry about when I hear the house settling."

Chastain giggles. "But seriously, when are you leaving?"

"I'm expecting to be on the road by three p.m. I'm almost done packing. You know you could come with me, get away from your life for a minute."

"No way! And leave all four kids with their dad? They wouldn't last ten minutes."

"Now who sounds like they need to get away? You're in total denial. Those four kids are going to eat you alive, and what'll be left of my beautiful friend?"

"Shut up. I'm fine. I'm waiting for Val to be fully potty-trained before I allow myself freedom. It took four hours to get my hair done last month. I left Chris to watch her. So much for potty-training. It was two weeks before she was back to where we are now. I'm so close to having a diaper-free household."

"Okay, Super Mommy. You know best."

"Ha-ha. Stay safe, and remember to keep in touch."

"I will, Chas. Love you."

"Love ya, bye."

I hang up the phone and stare at the ceiling of my bedroom before slowly turning and sitting up, putting my feet on the cool laminate flooring. I look out the window and breathe out a sigh, anxiety at the pit of my stomach. I exhale deeply, trying to expel the image of the woman in my dream. *Mei, why now?*

CHAPTER 1:

FIVE DAYS BEFORE LAKE LURE

The yoga studio is packed full of young hipsters. I get a whiff of incense as I walk in, and it makes the wide-open space feel sacred, yet foreign. Foreign from any other bustling business in Atlanta. Getting a taste of it a couple of times a month is all I can swing. It's the price I pay to be in the moment.

No natural light enters the studio, but a dim nightlight glow radiates from the ceiling. The heat is cranked up to hotter than hell.

I walk over to the community mats and grab one while dodging others doing the same. On top of the shelving for blocks, the incense billows out, creating free-form shapes moving through the room. I nab a block and find a spot.

Trying to clear my mind, I close my eyes and lie on my back with feet up and bent knees. The moment where I feel myself fully.

I hear hushed voices in the background, chattering, catching up before class. This time is for me. I don't know anyone in the class. It's better that way. I can pass through like I'm invisible. How long can I go with no one bumping into me, smiling my way, or talking to me? It's a game I play.

The instructor begins. The music is chants from India to a techno beat; it kicks in, and the volume increases. The heat acts as a medium to burn away my thoughts. The relief is welcome. I can't think of anything but the movement. Thirty-plus people are moving and breathing together. It doesn't take long before the sweat is pouring. As it trickles down my body, I feel my muscles warming and stretching. The synergy of movement among strangers overtakes me, as if the group movement is the brain behind the operation.

Then, like a comet, anxiety hits my heart, takes root, and spreads throughout my body. Emotion follows, and the room spins. I close my eyes and bury my face in the mat. My eyes swell, tears mingling with the sweat on my face. My heart pounds with grief, and the tears flow. *Focus on your breathing*, my therapist would say.

This happens too often, the marriage of sweat and tears. Here, no one asks me if I'm okay; no one knows. The disguise of red-faced sweat hiding swollen eyes and tears is my hidden outlet. Even if they could tell, they wouldn't care. I'm not like them.

Like I've been transported through time, the class ends. A damp towel is placed on my forehead, and the coldness and aroma of lavender and peppermint bring me back.

I slowly sit up in a cross-legged position with prayer hands.

"Take your intention with you throughout the day," ends the instructor. Namaste.

Just like that, our oasis is gone. The rush to leave is strong—back to the routine that pays the bills and keeps us all surviving. Back to reality.

The guy behind me is staring at me, and it catches me off guard. I look back—just a slight glance. Yep. The game's over. Someone noticed me. A mischievous smile crosses my face.

I spray off my mat, roll it up, and walk out. Cold air hits my body at once—relief.

I enter the common area and go to my cubby, put on my shirt and flip-flops. People are huddled in the lobby, everyone happy and relaxed, thanking the instructor for a great class.

There's that guy again. I see him from the corner of my eye, and I can feel his stare. I look over, catch him staring at me. He looks up and smiles—embarrassed, I guess. I watch him put on his shirt. He's got a runner's build, dark hair graying around the sides. *Not bad.*

Distraction is the next best thing to therapy, Dr. Nash told me at one of our sessions. *Try to distract yourself with things that make you feel good about yourself.* Mr. Runner's Build is a definite distraction.

I gather my confidence and ask, "Is this your first time here?" He seems surprised.

"Oh...yes. I just started coming to the Sunday class." He looks down while putting on his shoes and then looks back at me. "How about you?"

I grab the tiny purse that holds my phone, keys, and a few cards. "I come most Sundays. Miranda is a great instructor."

"She is good. It was hot as fuck in there." The word "fuck" rolled nicely from his mouth. I smile in agreement.

"The cold rag at the end is the best part by far."

He smirks. "Oh, man, it truly is. It's like being revived from death."

I laugh at that a little louder than I planned.

He pauses, looks over at me, then seems to come to a decision. "I'm dying for some coffee, and I have no plans this morning. Want to join me?"

I smile. *That was fast.* "Sure. Let me hit the restroom first." I fix my hair and put it up in a bun on top of my head. I have no makeup on, but that doesn't seem to matter.

I head outside the studio and find him waiting for me. I feel like we're meeting for the first time after an online dating match. "Sorry I didn't introduce myself. My name is Peter."

"Hi, Peter, I'm Emily. Do you know of a coffee shop close by?"

"Yes. I actually live walking distance from here, and there's a little coffee shop at the corner of my building."

"Perfect."

Thirty-five minutes later, we're fucking on his couch. We hadn't been able to make it to the bedroom. His loft apartment is in midtown Atlanta, wall-to-wall windows overlooking the skyline. The furniture is posh, with a minimalist style, walls brick with a rustic feel. Flooring is concrete, and the ceilings are twenty-something feet tall.

I should thank our yoga instructor for the sex. Our breathing rhythm was somehow in sync, already ingrained in muscle memory. Our bodies followed suit in a waltz—no hiding—emotions raw and exposed. I'm myself when I have sex, especially with strangers. They always thank me afterward, like it was about them or some favor. Funny, it's never about them.

Our quick chat before sex was casual and nice. He smiles a lot. I like that. He owns his own business and comes to one of his main offices in Atlanta one week per month. I also like that. His business is a tech company that has a technology that deals with an app...blah, blah, blah. He lost me about that time. I don't care. The details don't matter. He makes money, he owns or rents an apartment that he only lives in once a month. For this moment, it's hot to me and spontaneous...and frankly, distracts me from—me.

Afterward, it's always awkward—the talk. I grab the throw from the back of the couch and wrap it around me. I pick up my to-go coffee from where I left it on the side table and take a sip, then walk over to the window overlooking the city. *I could live here.*

His voice interrupts my musing. "Sorry, I didn't expect to have a guest today. I didn't really clean up or plan..."

I look around to see nothing is out of place except a computer and some files scattered on the island in the kitchen. He must feel awkward too. Small talk after something so personal is unnatural—a continuity issue.

I press my forehead to the window. "The city looks so old from here. I love it."

His voice lightens, relief at finding something he can talk about, I assume. "Oh, yeah... I fell in love with this location the moment I saw it. This is an old cotton mill turned into apartments. I couldn't believe the cost. Being from California, this is just..."

I hear him talking, but the euphoria of the moment is wearing off, and I no longer focus on what he's saying. Butterflies in my stomach turn into birds with strong wings flapping, trying to get out. A buzzing sound fills my ears. The sex was therapeutic, and now it's over.

His voice weaves its way back into my consciousness. "Can I ask you a question, Emily?"

I stay turned toward the window. "Yes."

He hesitates. "Why were you crying at yoga?"

I'm jolted by the realization that I'd been crying in public, not in private, and someone noticed. I suddenly feel naked, even though I've been naked all this time. I turn to face him as he lies on the couch. Agitation creeps up in me with this personal question.

I hit back with, "Are you regular, Peter? How many poops do you have in a day?"

He exhales on an unexpected laugh. "Okay," he responds. "Point taken. None of my business."

I turn back to the view of the city. I see in the window's reflection that Peter is coming up behind me. He places his arms around my waist after moving my long hair over my right shoulder. He presses his body up against mine like we know each other.

"Ummm," he says. "That was amazing." Wait for it. "Thank you for such a...wild coffee date. You were...on fire." And there it is.

The throw drops to my feet on the floor, my naked skin revealing what Peter really wants: a beautiful woman seasoned by his climax.

I watch the reflection of myself in the window, a middle-aged woman who has aged beautifully among her cohort. I should feel on top of the world right now, but I don't. I see him behind me, and his eyes move across the silhouette of my curves. He doesn't have to say it. I know what he's thinking. His appetite for me is written all over the reflection of his face. Some would say a gift; I would say a curse. Never really seeing me—my body masking the view of my soul. If you really pay attention, my essence reveals something else. I would be lying if I said I didn't enjoy the stares, the attention, the fact that I can evoke some sort of joy in another person, rather than the opposite.

I turn and give him a long, passionate goodbye kiss. He doesn't know this will be the last time he sees me. I look right into his eyes as I pull back. I'm about to say I have to go, that I have an appointment or something, when I see the tattoo on his neck that I didn't notice before. It's a small black butterfly. I wouldn't have pinned him as a butterfly tattoo kind of guy.

Intrigued, I ask, "A butterfly?"

He shrugs. "I got it in Japan. My mother passed away while I was there. She loved butterflies. And, well...I loved my mom."

At that, nausea sets in. The need to flee runs through every inch of my body. Although the apartment is spacious, I feel closed in, like I have no place to turn. My breath feels short. I can't get enough air into my lungs. My heart starts pounding, and the flapping of wings in my belly returns with intensity.

The need to save face encourages me to run out. Leave him thinking that I'm an interesting yet mysterious woman. That's the image I want. My magic trick, the tiny bit of control I have over this world—leave him wanting more.

My excuse is hasty. "Oh, shit. I just forgot that I have to take my best friend to her doctor's appointment." It isn't a good lie, but it works. I hurry over and put on my yoga clothes, their dampness slowing the process. They feel icky and cold, accentuating my uneasiness.

I flash a fake smile at Peter and move toward the door, but he reaches for my arm before I can reach it, a boyish look on his face. "Wait! Emily, your number. Can we have another coffee date sometime?"

I stop. I almost made it out. I turn and give him my cell phone number, one number off. Then I run the whole way to my car.

Sunday yoga will be switched to Monday yoga. Reset.

CHAPTER 2:

I'm staring at a blank canvas. Metamorphosis, my next exhibit, is only a little over two months away. I've been blocked before, but this is the worst. I don't have the right headspace, and I can't move forward with an idea.

I look up at my wall, at the sketches of Sienna that I drew and framed every three years from the time she was three to fifteen. My gaze goes to three-year-old Sienna. Chubby cheeks, a smile that rearranges her whole face, the twinkle in her eye, and a life force that would make you believe she could live forever.

She was three when I left her and Kyle. If I'd never left, would things have happened the same? At sixteen now, would I be chatting with her about someone she liked or wanted to date? Would she be telling me about the annoying girls in her school and how dramatic they are? Sharing secret jokes that only we could laugh at, that no one else would understand?

I take a sip of my coffee and realize it's cold. I debate reheating it or just getting a new cup altogether. A new cup it is. I go over to my one-cup-at-a-time coffeemaker, dump out the old grounds, and shovel a heaping mound into the coffee basket. Press Start.

I look around my apartment while I wait for it to brew. It feels frozen. Swivel chairs at the side bar don't swivel, cabinet doors remain shut. Only the harmony of the appliances steals the silence. No other energy or movement. Filled with a punishing solitude.

I'm grabbing the creamer out of the fridge when I hear a knock at the door and look out the window. It's my landlord, Susan, who catches me peering out the window and waves. Susan and Tim are recent empty-nesters. I live above their three-car garage in an eight-hundred-square-foot apartment. I've been dodging her for a while now. Braless and still in my pajamas, I race to my closet to find a cardigan.

Wrapping it around me, I answer the door. "Hi, Susan, how are you?"

Susan smiles, then her face transforms to a look of concern. I've grown accustomed to seeing this pattern.

"Hi, Emily. I'm good. I've been trying to talk to you for weeks now, but we somehow keep missing each other. Did you get the messages I left you?"

I pretend not to know what she's talking about. "Um...no, I didn't. I'm horrible at checking my messages."

She furrows her brow. "Oh. Well, I just wanted to know if your toilet got cleared last month."

"Yes, it did. Thank you for the help."

Susan pauses and stares at me for a few awkward seconds.

"Anything else, Susan?" I can see her look past me to the kitchen and notice how messy the place is. The judgment I sense burns through me.

Susan makes a face like there was something else she wanted to say, but she lost her train of thought. "Oh, yes. The whole reason I came over. You paid last year's rent all in one lump sum, but I just wanted to remind you that the year was up a month ago, and I haven't received your rent payment. You don't have to pay us yearly. Month to month is fine."

There it is—the moment I was dreading. I pretend like I've forgotten. "Oh, crap. I keep forgetting to get it to you. I'm so sorry. I'll send you the money right now for three months. Hopefully, I can pay for the rest of the year after my exhibit in a couple of months."

I grab my phone while she waits and log into my account. I don't have enough to cover one month, let alone three. I look up at her and flash a nervous smile. *Shit, I'll have to dig into my savings.*

I make the transfer into my checking account, but Susan is getting anxious.

"I know you're good for it, Emily. I'm just gonna go. I've got to grab Tim's medication at the drugstore." She turns and leaves.

I send Susan three months' worth of rent, feeling the sting as the money exits my account. No problem. I can eat black beans and rice for days in a row without getting tired of them. I even like them better knowing that each meal costs me next to nothing.

Although the money hurts going out, I'm relieved to know that I owe one less thing. I wonder what type of person is set up for feast or famine.

I grab my coffee, and it's cold again. I reheat it in the microwave and head back to my studio.

Back to the drawing board—my blank canvas. It's as if the need for money squashes my imagination. The stress of needing to pay everyday bills discourages my creative mind at the worst moments. I close my eyes and try to clear my thoughts and see what comes.

The blankness in my mind reflects on the canvas. Nothing going on, and nothing worth it. All that keeps cycling through my mind are generic rushes of butterflies, fluttering around and around through my head. The butterflies don't stop on anything interesting. Nothing unique to the eye or different, nothing out of the ordinary, nothing ordinary that might be an unnoticed spectacle. They don't change or transform; they just stay the same, an endless cycle of the same, no progression.

It's no use. I open my eyes. Butterflies are insects that people adore because they transform into something beautiful from something that was ordinary. Not only do they transform into something stunning, but they go from a slow crawl to flying at a hundred times the speed they could travel before. It's a symbol of hope and change to something not only better, but spectacular. Without the transformation, the butterfly is nothing but a pretty bug where magic and the possibility of something greater don't exist.

Frustrated, I pick up my paintbrush and paint a gigantic black butterfly. It resembles what a child would paint: simple and imperfect. I stare at it for several minutes.

Disappointed, I jump off my stool and go to the kitchen for lunch. I grab a Maruchan ramen packet, and ten minutes later, I have steamy broth and ramen noodles in a bowl. The pot gets chucked into the sink, banging against the rest of the unwashed dishes.

I carry the bowl back to my studio and sit down on my stool. I twirl the noodles around my fork and shovel them into my mouth. I swallow, and as the noodles travel down to my belly, I realize how famished I am. I hungrily eat the rest, then put the bowl up to my mouth and drink the broth, all while staring at the painting. I put the bowl aside, and with slow intent, I carefully paint over the butterfly, creating a large black cube, making the edges of the cube as straight and perfect as I can. Paint fills the empty spaces to where the butterfly is no longer discernible to the eye. I know it's there—a boxed butterfly, forever trapped. I take in the painting for a minute. Then I grab it from the easel and throw it on the floor. It lands with a thud and skids. The action wasn't as cathartic as I'd hoped. Irritated, I think, *I'm the trapped butterfly*.

CHAPTER 3:

I'm waiting for my friend and gallery owner, Arin Wang, at a trendy restaurant alongside the Atlanta Beltline. We're supposed to go over my work for the Metamorphosis exhibit. As usual, she's running late.

The hostess seats me at a table on the back patio. It's March, a month where Georgians have learned to throw weather expectations out the window. It could be sleeting, or you could fry up some bacon on your back porch. The sun is out, and the temperature is in the seventies, an ideal spring day that attracts the flocks of people strolling by. I scan the menu and order the most expensive glass of pinot noir. Because of Arin. She pays attention to these sorts of details.

Arin and I met each other through Chastain. I was desperate after my divorce to sell my artwork and make a living. I wanted to be self-sufficient, to pull my financial weight for Sienna. Chas introduced us, and I've been a sideliner watching Arin and her glamorous life ever since. Not only that, but she sells my art for a lot more than I would have ever dreamed.

A trust-fund baby who didn't waste her good fortune by idling away her time, instead she used it to her advantage and made an exhilarating and noteworthy life for herself.

Arin always seems to have her life together. She can easily detect what people's issues are, and she always has a solution—well, Arin's solution. That's what I don't like about Arin. She says it's the constant work she does on herself. Seeing a therapist twice a week combined with trips to exotic places. She feels her lifestyle choices and teachings afford her the opportunity to point out everyone's flaws and resolve them for them. It's completely demoralizing, but I can't hate Arin—no one can. You can only hate that you love her.

Arin made a success of her gallery using her money and connections. She searches for unique pieces of art as she travels around the world, staying in places like meditation sanctuaries, yoga retreats, and monasteries with monks. She finds reclusive locations, places in the jungle or Indigenous villages, to get an authentic, rich experience. Sometimes she showcases her photography alongside the items she collects. She writes about her experience of the culture and then displays the art pieces. She's great at selling them, tells the backstory, shows pictures of Native artists at work, and talks passionately about the meaning and effort involved in the process. Arin exudes confidence. It's the only thing I envy about her. Nothing else.

Arin isn't married and doesn't have kids. She confessed to me once that she didn't really need a man or a woman. She told me, laughing, "I don't want anyone tying me down or changing my goals in life. Maybe I'm just selfish, but at least I know it."

I'd joked, "At least all you have to worry about is yourself. True happiness, with no other complications." She hadn't laughed, just ignored what I said.

Arin doesn't ask me what's going on with me. Ever. She never brings up Sienna. Really, I think she's bored by kids. She doesn't want them, so why would she care about anyone else's? She doesn't really talk to me about my life. She only talks about what she notices in front of her face: my dress, what I order, my mood, and my fucking aura. However, I know about her entire life. I know what she likes to drink, what diet she's currently on, how her dad died when she was in second grade, and how her mom remarried a wealthy business investor less than three months later. I know how many times a week her cleaner comes to her house, what brand of toilet paper she buys, when she has a lover in her life, and when she doesn't.

I see Arin from the entrance, and I'm suddenly nervous. *Shit, should I have ordered a glass of wine for her too? Ugh...too late.*

Arin, an Asian American beauty, makes her entrance wearing a long, sleek dress in a beige crochet style, very hobo-chic. It barely covers her goods, but since Arin is slender with a petite frame, she gets away with it. A gaudy, green stone necklace embraces her neck and contrasts against her tanned skin. Her entire ensemble was likely purchased during her last trip, a respectful tribute to the culture and experience. Her curled hair bounces as she walks. Sunglasses cover half her face, and she has on a straw beach hat. She stands out. She always stands out.

When she heads over to my table, she shouts, "Well, hello, my long-lost friend. How are you?" Her casual stride makes her look as if she's exhausted, as though she's walking into her own home after a long day's work at the office, which is hardly the case.

I stand up, step toward her, and trip on the leg of my chair, catching myself on the table before I fall. Ignoring the mishap, she gives me a kiss on the cheek. At this moment I feel like she thinks I'm her best friend, even though she doesn't know if I live with my parents or in a mansion in Buckhead.

"How have you been, my friend?" She looks at my glass of wine, and before I can answer says, "Oh, that looks good. What is it?"

Prepared, I say, "It's the Pinot Noir, Left Coast Estate Cuvee, I believe. It's good. Do you want a taste?"

"Well, of course." She takes a sip. "Ummm. It is good." But she makes a face like it's bad. "It's not what I'm feeling right now, though. I just got back from Tulum, Mexico. I stayed in this adorable beach bungalow. They had THE best margaritas." She pauses. "No, I'm feeling more like a cocktail. Em, you always go with the same old drink. Add some variety to your palate."

Last time, when I asked for the house wine, she told me that I should go for the best glass of wine on the menu. *What you put in your body should be the best and of the utmost quality. Quit underestimating what you deserve.*

Looking at the menu she says, "I'm going for the Elder Rosa." She immediately flags down a waiter and gives her drink order.

Arin and I are a completely different species of human. I wonder why she even hangs out with me. I'm not quite certain why I agree to meet her for these outings where we talk two percent business and ninety-eight percent her adventurous, amazing life, and how my life is sad and wrong.

"So, Arin, how was Tulum? I'm sure it was fantastic."

"Oh, yes. It was. And there was Edwardo, an intense romantic local." She removes her sunglasses and raises her eyebrows with a smile. "We spent twenty-four hours straight smoking pot and making love. I did a cleansing with a Mayan witch doctor. Found some great genuine Mayan artists, and ate my way through pounds of the best seafood. It was so wonderful. I feel refreshed."

She laughs deeply, and it sounds rehearsed as if she's practiced to get it exactly how she wants it. "There's nothing like being somewhere completely foreign, feeling the discomfort of it after the novelty wears off, then returning to your life as you know it—the comfort, routine, everything. You appreciate it so much more. You know what I'm talking about, Em?"

I don't know what she's talking about. I try to remember the last trip I took anywhere, let alone to a foreign country. I think it was a resort in Jamaica when I was still married to Kyle, and that was over thirteen years ago.

"Yes, I do. That's so awesome, Arin. Glad you had such a great time."

"Oh, Em, your aura is looking so sad and drab. I feel this heavy energy coming from you. Life is wearing you down."

Here we go again. She pauses and changes her tone. "How's the artwork coming along for the Metamorphosis exhibit?"

"I haven't been able to focus lately, and I can't get going with this project. I'm not quite sure what's blocking me."

"You need exactly what I just came back from. You need to refresh. Get lost and find yourself again. Go to Mexico, Egypt, Italy. Go someplace that moves you. Get your inspiration from being alone and free." Her voice rises and falls as if she's preaching and wants everyone in the restaurant to hear what she has to say. Like everyone has her money and freedom by default, and why don't they just, well, take advantage of it?

As she's speaking, I stare at her through my long-stemmed wineglass. Her face is distorted and blurred, which helps take the edge off what she's saying, blunting the advice that's realistic for her, yet so unrealistic for me.

The remaining wine isn't worth another throwback of the glass. Getting another one will help take the edge off Arin even more. "Arin, you want another drink?"

"Oh, no. I actually need to go and entertain some art collectors. They just called me three hours ago; said they're passing through on their way home and would love to meet up. Why they only gave me three hours' notice is beyond me."

I see the waiter and order another glass of wine, then I turn to Arin. "Why didn't you tell them you can't meet them? That you had other plans."

"I would never, ever, in a million years pass up a chance to entertain art collectors. Haven't I taught you anything? And now that I'm thinking about it... Oh my God, why didn't I think of this before? Come with me and help me entertain them. It would be a great opportunity for you to make connections. You never know, they could come back to the Metamorphosis exhibit and buy up all your artwork. Or bring their friends."

I take a sip of my wine. I know she's right, but it's the last thing I want to do. However, showing my face and schmoozing some collectors could mean paying rent for a year, one less thing to stress about. "Okay, Arin, I'll go with you. It sounds like a good opportunity."

"Yay! It'll be fun. You'll see." Arin finishes off her drink. "So, Em, where can I book your next flight? Because you're getting out of town. I want this exhibit to be the best one you've had yet. Something to do with nature and the metamorphosis of time. And I'm not talking about butterflies. If you paint a damn butterfly, I'm going to toss it out."

I laugh at that. "Arin, I can't take all my art supplies on a plane. I'm not going to fly anywhere."

"Okay, then drive somewhere. Go to the mountains; go to North Carolina."

"Why North Carolina?"

"I don't know why I said North Carolina. It just came out. I mean, they have mountains there, right?"

"I don't know."

"Quit being so stubborn. You're so ridiculous. Is it money? I can fund the trip, you know."

"I know you can fund the trip, but you already sell my art. You're not going to pay for my inspiration trip. I won't let you."

"When are you going to think about Emily? This is what I'm talking about. Your energy is so sad; it's like you can't see how weighted down you are. Do something different and for yourself."

"Okay, I'll think about it. I promise."

Arin winks at me and smiles. "Why don't we get going? You can follow me back to my house. I have plenty of lovely wine to drink. Better than the one you're drinking, I promise."

I roll my eyes when she looks down at her purse and chug the rest of my glass of wine. We pay the bill, and I follow her out.

In my car on the way over to Arin's, there's something not right in my gut. Anxiety with no reason is annoying. You can't think your way out of it. My choice for the evening will be more wine—self-medication at its best. Bottoms up.

CHAPTER 4:

I've been to Arin's house so many times in the past thirteen years that it's almost a second home to me. It's huge, with cathedral ceilings on each floor. She needs the space; not for Arin, but for her enormous art collection. The inside of her house looks like a museum of anthropology. But it lacks a sense of comfort, a lived-in feel. It's more like a cold, hard, aloof atmosphere. Good for entertaining, gatherings, and intellectual discussions. The openness invites my anxiety, provides no outlet to hide, no blankets to protect my body or softness to counteract the exposure. It's not for sleeping, cooking, or lying on the couch to watch TV. I can't even picture Arin doing those things.

The first piece of artwork you see when you enter her house is a painting of Arin when she went to her first meditation retreat with monks in Nepal. She wasn't allowed to speak to anyone for a month. I painted it from a picture she gave me that someone took of her doing her daily sunrise meditation. She's sitting cross-legged with palms up and her eyes open. The sun is rising in the back, and she's framed by the monastery. She sits on the stoop at the front entrance, and you can see all the way to the open back entrance, to the rising sun. She'd explained that the routine was difficult to adapt to and that the mornings were the worst part of the day.

I've painted several pictures from her trips for her. Arin enjoys my paintings because she says that I'm good at capturing the soul of the people I paint; I paint their humanity. She raves about this painting. I captured her vulnerability at that time. She had gone through some deep emotional pain and couldn't talk to anyone about it—she just did her meditations and chores, day in and day out. Through that process, she met her demons and found a way to expel them—a triumph that was memorialized in this painting.

As she sits there in a brave meditative pose, shoulders back, eyes filled with hardness and darkness, in the background is a person on hands and knees scrubbing the floor. This person is also Arin, giving servitude. It was originally a separate picture someone had taken of her. She loved the melding of the two, thanked me for capturing it.

Arin lives about five minutes away from the restaurant in an up-and-coming bougie neighborhood in the Old Fourth Ward. I open her front door and walk inside. She meets me at the entrance with two glasses of wine in hand and hands me one of the glasses. "Here, try this. It will blow your fucking mind." She makes a mind-blowing gesture with her free hand.

Arin turns and walks into the living room, and I follow. The lighting in the house isn't coming from electricity, but from hundreds of lit tea candles. The glow is brilliant. I'm certain Arin didn't light all the candles herself. I'm sure she asked her assistant, Gail, at the last minute to light them while she was enjoying drinks with me. Arin loves it when people notice her spectacles, so I always stroke her ego. "Holy shit, Arin, the candles are stunning. You did this all for two art collectors?"

She looks back at me and rolls her eyes. *Silly me for thinking such rubbish.* "No...I had it set up for a large gathering before I went to Mexico. All we had to do was light them again. We might as well get use out of them. It took forever to set them all up. Everything and everyone looks so much more interesting in candlelight, right?"

We enter the kitchen. Several mismatched platters with different textures are cradling appetizers on an oversize kitchen island.

I bring the wineglass to my nose, smell it, and take a sip. The wine hits my tongue with silky smoothness. It's lovely, but I won't admit it to Arin.

She looks at me. "Yeah, see what I mean? Now you're happy you came. I'm not here to disappoint." She laughs at herself. "So those guys just texted me; they're on their way over... Grab some snacks, Em."

I grab some cheese and crackers in one hand and my wine in the other, then follow Arin into the living room where she grabs her phone, points it at the fireplace, and *poof*, a fire appears. She taps her phone again, and music turns on. She has a large candlelit chandelier in the center of the living room, enveloping the room in an amber glow. Underneath the chandelier in front of the fireplace is a low-backed, mid-century-looking couch. It looks like something West Elm would sell, but I would never say that to Arin. Her furniture is all antiques from some off-the-beaten-path store or shipped from some faraway country. Every piece of furniture, art, knickknack, is well thought out. Nothing is an impulsive purchase; it takes hours of meditation or several contemplative nights to make the decision. It's just as obnoxious as her money—the time she spends deciding such things.

As I walk through, I stop at a piece in the living room. It's a sliver of a tree stump turned upright. The grain of the wood is brought out by the stain, and the bark on the outside edge is still intact. A sculpture of a naked woman is attached to its surface, her arms thrown up, hair tousled, eyes closed, with a confident smile on her face. The artist titled it *Free*.

I've admired this piece several times before, but at this moment, the amber lighting offers a different emotion. The sentiment is of a devilish apparition coming out to show pleasure, an untamed woman—something forbidden and wrong. Before, I thought it virtuous, but now it feels bewitching.

The music is upbeat, an African drumbeat encouraging an energetic alertness. I hear it cranking up, and I turn my attention to Arin. She's stomping to the beat with a half march, half dance, as she struts around setting things up. I laugh and shake my head to myself. *She's happy.* Jealousy stings my heart.

Arin does a similar setup with her gallery shows, setting a notable ambience. She says it helps take the pressure and edge off the customers and artists. "You offer an unforgettable atmosphere, as if it's its own piece of art, along with great food and wine, and voilà—they don't know what hit them, so they want to purchase more artwork."

For one of her shows, she'd purchased truckloads of white sand and had two inches of it covering the flooring of her gallery. Everyone had to take off their shoes to walk through it and view the artwork, drink, and mingle. Every piece of art had been purchased within two hours. The exhibit had been scheduled for two nights. Since the art had all sold in one, the next night was a 1950s beach-style dance party.

I met an attractive twenty-something the night of the dance party who had a great taste in music. He went on and on about one of my paintings that hadn't been purchased from a prior exhibit. My buzz had me hanging on to his lean biceps in his wifebeater, mooning over his tight jean shorts and perfect smile. Later that night, I was flat-out drunk, and fucking this man was all I could think about. So I took his hand and led him to the smallest room of the gallery, shut the door, and locked it. We started standing up, and then we fell onto the sand and rolled around, finishing together, me on top, him cupping my breasts. Afterward, I stumbled out of the gallery into my Uber with sand up my ass. Arin and Chastain high-fived me the next day.

We sit down on her couch where she begins to tell me about the collectors. She's already changed her attire to something more conventional: a button-down shirt with hand stitching on it and some tight blue jeans. I look at my generic black dress from Old Navy, and it feels like a B movie compared to her blockbuster outfit.

Arin takes a long sip of her wine and begins. "So, George and Mariam, they're a married southern White couple who have been collecting twentieth-century American art since the seventies. They own a gallery in South Georgia. Your stereotype of a snobby art collector will literally be challenged." Arin changes her neutral accent to a more southern one. "They're southern as southern gets." She giggles. "They are adorable. You won't see George without a cigar in his mouth, even as he talks. It's just as impressive as his art collection."

I take a long sip of my wine before replying. "I love them already."

Just as I'm about to ask another question, the doorbell rings. Anxiety shoots through my heart as Arin jumps up. "Just be yourself, and maybe add a bit of...confidence, you know, about your art." She winks at me.

There it is, a reminder, once again, of how I appear to the outside world. My anxiety heightens, and I feel it circulating in my gut. I tip my glass of wine back and gulp the rest of it down, then go into the kitchen to serve myself another. The buzz has already numbed my head, adding some pseudo-confidence.

I can hear Arin talking to the collectors in the foyer. The up and down of voices becomes louder and clearer as they walk closer. They're distracted by the artwork, statues, and paintings along the way, and it takes them several minutes to reach the kitchen. I'm picking at cheese and crackers and taking quick sips of wine—too quick to enjoy the caliber to its fullest.

When they reach the kitchen, Arin does her over-the-top introduction of me to put me on a fake pedestal. "And this, my friends, is Emily, my beautiful friend and fabulous painter."

She says this as she puts her arm around me and kisses my cheek. I smile, and my cheeks warm. I nod to them. "Nice to meet you."

They tell me their names, and I try to match their accents as I speak, going back to my roots. "Arin has some interesting pieces; I think it took y'all an hour to get here from the time you entered the house."

Mariam and George laugh, and their laughter echoes throughout the house. My mind disengages from the group interaction, giving space from me to them.

Mariam turns to me. "Arin showed us one of your paintings. George and I really like your style. It's a good painting of Arin in Nepal, and I love the merging of the servitude piece. I remember seeing those pictures on Instagram when Arin took that trip. I feel like you really captured the feeling of the experience."

Mariam's words pull my mind back to the here and now. "Arin's experiences make it easy to paint. I would love to follow her around and paint every moment."

Arin gasps. "Oh, you bitch. Did you see what she did there? First of all, I'll say thank you for her. Why must you say such bullshit?"

Laughing, I reply, "What? It's totally what I think; it's so true." I look at Mariam and George. "Wouldn't you want to have Arin's life?"

Arin isn't giving up, though. She continues. "But…that's not what makes the painting good. You listen and see things that others don't and bring them to the forefront in a different perspective."

I know at this point I'm in a corner, and Arin won't let me out. "Okay, jeez. Thank you. I'm not going to win this one."

Mariam laughs and says, "However, Emily is right. I wouldn't mind being in Arin's shoes. Nice try, Arin. Now I got you."

Our laughter thunders through the walls, and the echoes hang on a little longer, blunting some of the conversation. It's another distraction. My brain falters for a moment, focusing on vacant sounds and not the point of this interaction. My heart quickens.

Shit, too much drink has got me turned around. Or is it something else?

Arin's voice pulls me back. "All right, I've got this killer wine that everyone must try. Who wants a glass?" She looks over to the bottle of wine that she opened earlier and notices that it's only got half a glass left in it. She gives me a devilish smile and shakes her head. "Please excuse me. I need to run and grab another bottle from the wine chest. Seems we're really enjoying this one."

While Arin runs to get the wine, I ask Mariam and George, "So where are you coming from? Arin told me you were passing through from somewhere else."

George replies with his cigar sticking out of his mouth, which causes him to have a throaty voice, increasing the novelty of his southern drawl. "We were visiting some friends in Asheville. They own a gallery there."

Just as he says that, Arin comes back with a bottle in hand. But now, all I can focus on is George's cigar, its size growing larger.

"Asheville!" Arin smiles. "That's perfect for you, Em."

I'm brought back to the point. I must focus on the point and stay in the natural pattern of conversation. It's so easy to play along. It's ingrained; it's autopilot.

"Oh yeah. Arin was just telling me to go to North Carolina to get away and paint for inspiration. I'm in a rut."

Mariam looks up with thoughtful eyes. "Asheville is cool, but a better place for inspiration is an hour outside of Asheville in a town called Lake Lure."

Words are getting shorter and running together a bit. The volume is off. I hear loudness and then softness in their voices.

George adds, "Mari and I loved it. Our friends own a cabin there, and we stayed with them for a weekend. We loved it so much, we even checked out real estate before we left."

"You can hike, and there's a little town there. It's adorable."

"Well, Em, looks like you found your spot," Arin says. She

looks over at me and mouths *You'd better go*, and then turns back to the others. "Okay, friends, let's venture into the living room so we can relax in front of the fireplace." Arin grabs an appetizer tray in each hand and heads to the living room.

I need a break; I can't breathe. "I need to use the bathroom. I'll meet y'all in the living room."

In the bathroom, I look at myself in the mirror in the glow of the mini candlelit chandelier above my head. I take lip gloss out and apply it, realizing just how tipsy I am as I press my lips together to blot the gloss.

I pee for what seems like an eternity. I grab the soap to wash my hands and notice an expensive scent that I like. I glance back up at my reflection and see an image of someone else; another woman, not me. My reflection has dark hair with small, coal-black eyes instead of my dirty-blond hair with large blue eyes. My heart rate quickens, and I pull my hands up to my face and touch it. My hands don't move in the mirror. I go for a long blink and open my eyes to see my reflection as it should be. I touch my face again, and the reflection mirrors my image. There it is. I'm okay, I didn't see Mei in the mirror. It was me, end of story.

I lean toward the mirror and look at myself. "Get it together, Emily. This is not going to happen. Get it together." I stare at myself until my heart settles and my breathing is back to normal. I feel better.

I leave the bathroom, but instead of going straight through the hallway, I turn back toward the kitchen to grab some food.

As I make the turn into the kitchen, I overhear Arin talking alone to Mariam in a hushed voice. They're huddled by some artwork just before the living room; their backs are toward me, and they don't know I'm there. I can't make out what they're saying, but their hushed tone strikes me as odd. I grab some stuffed olives and toss them in my mouth.

Arin's demeanor indicates it's a serious conversation—intent and secretive, hushed, so others can't make out the dialogue. I hear Arin say, "...Sienna. She refuses to talk to us. I can only imagine what...." I hear a mumble of words I can't make out. Stunned at what I just heard, I see Mariam nodding her head with concern.

As I stand there, my blood starts to boil. Why is Arin discussing something so personal about me with an art collector behind my back? What's her point? Is she playing the *poor Emily* card to sell my paintings? Is she using my shitty life story to make Mariam feel sorry for me? What a crock of shit!

Annoyed, I walk over, startling them with my presence.

Arin has an uncomfortable look on her face. "Oh, Em, there you are. Did you get some food?"

I'm caught off guard because I've never caught Arin off guard before. I've never seen her in an embarrassing situation. I ignore her question. "What were you just talking about? I heard Sienna's name."

Arin stumbles to find words. "Um...Em...well, Mariam was talking about how she and George are...getting a minivan for all the road trips they're taking and how people think they're crazy to want such a big car for just two people."

Mariam chimes in, "Yeah, people think we're so weird."

Mariam's a horrible liar. Shit. "It just sounded like a more serious chat than about cars."

Arin shook her head. "Nope, about cars. So, Em, did you try the Brie with some rosemary crackers? It's so good."

She walks into the kitchen, and Mariam follows. I can tell she's trying to get out of the conversation. I follow them because I'm not going to let this go.

"No, I didn't try the damn rosemary crackers."

The anger is fuming in my belly. I want to vomit my stuffed olives all over Mariam and Arin. I know they're lying.

"Arin, why were you talking about Sienna? I'm not a charity case! Are you using my tragedy to sell art?"

I realize my mouth is saying too much. I'm shocked at the words being expelled from it. Tears form in my eyes. I can't stop them, and soon they're streaming down my face.

The look on Arin's face shows her surprise. This is the first time I've ever seen her shocked. Arin looks at Mariam, who looks stunned and concerned at the same time. They stand there staring at me, and the energy turns cold.

Arin raises her hands to me. "Hold on, Em. No one is talking about Sienna. Please calm down."

"Arin, tell the truth. I'm not going to stand here and listen to this. You were talking about Sienna." My mouth is moving, and I have no control of what comes out of it.

Arin begins, "Okay, Em, I was talking about Sienna—"

I interrupt her. "Why would you lie, and why were you talking about Sienna? I've never heard you mention her name to my face. How messed up is that?"

Arin's face saddens and her posture slumps. "Because of this exact reaction. No one can bring her up without this…this reaction."

I'm so full of rage my mind can't think straight. "What? So you tell art collectors, so they know a tragic story about the artist? How convenient to have me around so you have something dramatic to talk about. What's the point? To sell art, or to feel better about yourself?"

Arin's hands fall to her sides, and she looks at Mariam, who turns to me. "No, Emily. Arin is like a daughter to me. She tells me personal things. I feel—"

I cut her off. "You feel sorry for me? Hey, everyone, look at the artist who didn't mother her daughter."

Arin reaches a hand toward me. "There's still a way to heal the…"

"Oh, Arin, I don't have the luxury of lying on a couch every other day and paying a professional to deal with a fart that came out wrong."

Mariam twitches. I think she laughed and tried to hide it.

Arin's face stiffens. "You think your problems are more important than mine? You think dealing with the death of my father was easy?"

"No, I just mean it's tons easier if you have money. That's all."

Arin's voice hardens. "I could just use the money to surround myself with crap and do drugs to numb the pain like other people I know. But I don't. I face it, and it feels like shit, Em."

I see tears forming in Arin's eyes. She's trying to hold them back, and there's a strength in her that petrifies me and softens me at the same time. I feel vulnerable and alone, backed into a corner that I can't get out of. I know she's been through tough experiences. Am I really saying hers are nothing in comparison to mine? Where do I run? How can I retract what I said? I want to see her money as a fault of hers, use her privileged life as a reason for shame.

Arin just shakes her head. "Em, I'm sorry for talking about Sienna behind your back. I can understand how that would make you upset. Please do me a favor and talk to a therapist about what happened."

Her apology seems backhanded, asking me to talk to a therapist. I look at Mariam, and I want to punch the *concerned/I'm here for you* look off her face. I know at this point the best response is to accept Arin's apology and move on. She did seem genuine in the apology part, but what can I expect from Arin? She always finds a way to be above it all, all-knowing.

I keep my voice neutral. "Thank you for apologizing." But my emotions are bizarre and wacky, the tears still streaming down my face. It's a mixed cocktail of anger, hurt, embarrassment, and sadness.

Arin looks at me. "Em, please go see your therapist. It's not healthy, the way you're handling it. I care about you, and I'm worried."

My anger neutralizes itself, and embarrassment is now coming in first place. I'm weak and feel alone in my grief.

Just as I'm about to speak, George walks up. He looks at me awkwardly. I imagine he was standing out in the living room listening to my outburst of emotion and trying to decide when the right moment would be to walk in.

How embarrassing. I just made a real fool of myself and ruined my chance with these art collectors. I'm done. Everything was going well, and now I'm looking at an audience of concerned onlookers. *Look at the poor starving artist. She's got a story to her, and it's so sad.* I picture other people I know talking about me when I'm not there. Shaking their heads. *It's so tragic, what a shame. She could have done this, but she didn't. Why didn't she just do that? I don't get it. What a shame.*

I apologize to everyone for my outburst. Arin offers to call her personal driver to drive me home in my car. I agree. It's time.

At home, I collapse on my bed and pick up the phone to call Dr. Nash. I leave a message to schedule an appointment. *Fucking Arin.*

CHAPTER 5:

I'm in the waiting room of Dr. Nash's office where boredom becomes your friend. You don't know whether to catch up on emails, look at a magazine, or watch the endless episodes of Dr. Phil on TV. Perhaps they think the long waits to get into the office are buffered by the extra advice that Dr. Phil can provide before sessions, a twofer. But today, something else is on the screen, and it catches my attention.

The show host, Vanessa Willis, introduces her guest. "Please welcome Dr. Pearl Jones. She is a psychologist and author of several books, and she's here to discuss her latest one—*Everyone is Crazy: How Society Feeds Mental Illness*."

Vanessa hugs Dr. Jones, and they take seats on the couch. "So I'm sure everyone is wondering what you mean by this book title. Everyone is crazy? I mean, we use the term loosely and call people crazy all the time, but what do you really mean?"

Dr. Jones shifts in her chair and smirks. "I mean, everyone is crazy."

Vanessa looks at the audience and laughs. The audience laughs along, then quiets to hear her response.

Dr. Jones says, "I define the term crazy to mean the opposite of healthy being, so I'm using it broadly."

"Okay, so I see how that can include everyone as crazy in those terms, but why use such a heavy word, such a broad meaning?"

"To explain the absurdity of how our culture literally trains us to be mentally unhealthy. It leads to clinical insanity for some, and for others, internal problems that show themselves in various ways: addictions to food, work, and substances. Insecurities about being able to survive successfully. These are all ways of sustaining mental health imbalance."

"So when people go clinically insane, you're saying it's all because of our society in the United States?"

"Crazy is a judgmental word that I know most will take offense to. I picked it to get people's attention. Not to judge the individual, but to hold accountable the larger societal constructs that are pushing us to go insane. If you aren't aware and you follow the societal rules, they're incredibly damaging to the human psyche. In a nutshell, the unconscious messaging in US culture is to work long hours to get paid more, sacrifice time raising your children, only take one vacation a year, spend all your money on childcare and a house, buy new cars and stuff to feel happy and cooler than your neighbor, eat foods high in fat, sugar, and salt, drink alcohol to relieve stress, and take a pill to deal with your emotions. Neighbors, the media, jobs, and our friends are all reinforcing the message. The cost of raising children is ridiculous; higher education is outrageous. If everyone blindly follows, they'll have breakdowns, psychotic episodes, suicides, turn to substances, create financial hardships, and go to a psychiatrist to get a pill to make it all better."

"You're painting a pretty grim picture of our culture. Is there any way to avoid the messaging, or to be aware, so people can avoid going crazy, or is crazy just what we are, and we don't have a choice in the matter?"

"Your genetic makeup and your family life as you grew up can work together to either buffer or enhance societal pressures. I would say if you were lucky and grew up in a high-functioning family that taught you how to deal with stress, money management, etc., then I think you'll have a better chance. It's not absolute."

"So how is our culture feeding mental illness?"

"What people need to understand in this culture is that it's driven by money, power, and an ideology of freedom. What happens is brainwashing of a sort, to think that money and power don't influence our freedom and that we're protected. But you're not protected from the constructs that are formed within this materialistic system. The drive for money to the point of greed and the results that spin off it can bring you to your knees psychologically. I'm simply here to tell you that this is happening, and being aware can push you to gain the tools that will help you manage it."

"What would you say to America are the takeaways from your book?"

"The first step is being aware of how our society affects your life personally. I want everyone to take a moment and notice the chaos. Just notice everything that must be done in your day. If you're a parent, this is especially important. List everything in your head, or write it down. Try to see it from the outside looking in, like it's not important, but it's what needs to get done. Realize that these are just things, and everything can be put off. Nothing is that important, and there is always a way around a problem or a challenge. You need to know that what your family, friends, social media feed, and media are telling you to do is not what you need to do. You need to listen to yourself and decide what's best for you to handle. Prioritize the BS. Get what you can done, and enjoy the rest of your time. Getting things done can feel empowering and good. If it doesn't, stop and regroup. Learn how to recognize when you can't handle something. Do not compare yourself to anyone else, because what someone else can do is not necessarily the same for you. Realize that these things we feel we have to do are really constructs that our society has created for us to be concerned about. It's all made up. Nothing is more important than what you need to do for yourself and your family. And repeat after me: *Everyone can just eff off.*"

Where was this psychologist thirteen years ago when I needed her? It would have resolved a lot of bullshit. I wouldn't be in this situation. I would have pushed through the rough spots; I would have understood that it wasn't just me who was going through it. The American dream isn't at all what it seems: the house, the marriage, the kids—it's all a mirage. So here I am now, Emily Black, with nothing to show for myself except what I thought was freedom. Only to find out that this is also a bunch of bullshit.

"Thank you for seeing me on such short notice, Dr. Nash," I say as she opens her office door.

"No problem at all. Someone canceled, so I had an opening."

I settle into my usual spot on the squishy couch across from her wingback chair and look up. She stares at me for a second through her large glasses before asking, "So what brings you in today?"

As if she didn't hear my voice message and didn't know the reason. "I liked what was on the TV in the waiting room before I came in."

"Oh really? What was Dr. Phil talking about today?"

"It wasn't Dr. Phil this time. It was a guest on Vanessa Willis's show. Dr. Jones."

"Oh, yes." She nods as if she knew that the incessant Dr. Phil shows the group practice had agreed to were going to be interrupted by a special episode from Vanessa Willis. "What did you like about it?"

"I don't know. I think that if I'd heard it thirteen years ago, I wouldn't have felt so alone, like I had reason to feel the way I did. Maybe I wouldn't have made the same choices in life. Maybe I wouldn't be here today."

"Well, I'm glad that it gave you a moment of self-reflection. Was it the interview where Dr. Jones talks about her book, *Everyone is Crazy*?"

"Yeah."

"I see. So how about we revisit what happened thirteen years ago?"

Through my many years of seeing therapists, psychologists, counselors, and psychiatrists, I learned how to get the most bang for my buck. "No, that's not why I'm here today." Don't waste time. You're paying her. When she goes somewhere you don't want to go, redirect her. I've already wasted ten minutes on my recent fascination with Dr. Jones. "I came here to talk about what happened at my friend Arin's house, like I said on your voicemail."

I explain again what happened. "Arin says she can't bring up Sienna to me, because every time she does, I get emotional."

"Do you agree with Arin?"

"I don't know… I don't remember a time when Arin brought up her name. It's almost like she never existed to Arin. I thought it was because kids weren't a part of her life. I was shocked when I heard Sienna's name come from her mouth."

"It sounds like she doesn't bring her up because of how you might respond. I mean, that's what she told you, right?"

"I guess."

"How about other friends? Could she be referring to how you respond with other mutual friends?"

"Maybe. She mentioned Chastain and how I won't talk about things. What do they want me to say?" I look out the window beside me to the parking lot of the building.

"Do you mind if I ask you a question, Emily?"

"Sure."

"Why don't you talk about what happened with Sienna to your friends? They're your support system, and they obviously care about you."

"They don't want to hear my sad story. Arin is too busy living the dream, and Chastain has four kids that she's a hundred and fifty percent invested in all the time. I don't want to remind them of how shitty I was as a mother. Perhaps…maybe, I'd lose them as friends."

I sit back. The on-point revelation I somehow was just able to verbalize shoots through my heart, and my eyes burn with tears.

"I think strongly that they don't feel the same about you. From what you've told me about your friends, they only want to be there and support you. Maybe you would help them both by being open. People need you to be truthful about your experience."

"How do you know that? I haven't even told you the whole story."

"No, you haven't told me the whole story." Dr. Nash looks at me with a straight face for a while. I know what she is doing, waiting for my response first, waiting for me to tell her the story.

"I was upset. I didn't even ask her what she was saying to Mariam."

"So you were upset because you heard Arin mention Sienna's name, not that she said something that offended you, correct?"

I shift in agitation. "She was talking behind my back, and then she lied about what she was talking about. I have every right to be upset about that."

"Just to be devil's advocate here, people say things behind people's backs all the time, and it doesn't have to always be something bad. Perhaps Arin was just telling Mariam about your daughter."

"If it wasn't anything bad, then why would she lie about it? It's obvious that she was saying something negative."

"Why did you have such an emotional response to it?"

Tears form in my eyes, and my heart pounds. Dr. Nash is not on my side with this. The feeling of frustration makes the tears come faster.

"Why doesn't anyone see how much pain I feel about the loss of Sienna?" The tears start rolling down my cheeks. I would understand it if they lost a child. I would understand it if they got emotional when I mentioned their child's name. Why is this not normal? I begin a new sentence, but I get choked up. I can't breathe.

Dr. Nash looks at me, concern evident on her face, and hands me a box of tissues. She waits for me to regain control of myself.

"We've been through this before. I'm beginning to feel strongly that your thoughts around Sienna are related to the trauma you experienced when you left your husband and her."

"That period of time is too much for me to think about. It took me years to look at myself in the mirror, and I'm still haunted by it."

"What you experienced was deep trauma. We need to back up and handle that experience first so we can make headway with Sienna."

The mention of the past feels like a blow to the head, like an insult. What a nasty little therapist. Emotions surge within my body from every direction possible. The emotional establishment of which is what and what is which is undiscernible. Frustration oozes out of my nostrils. My head's heating up, the pressure cooker is about to go off. Instead of an angry outburst, it's a parade of tears. Frustration…tears…frustration…tears. Find a way to move on from this moment. I finally manage to look at her. "I don't know how to handle not having Sienna in my life. How does a mother move on?"

Dr. Nash nods. "Let's talk about Sienna."

"No." I say, but I want to scream.

Dr. Nash's face goes stoic, and she looks down at her watch. She looks back up with a smile and says, "It looks like time is up. Are you staying on top of your meds?"

Frustrated, I nod. "Yes."

"Okay. Do you want to schedule something next week?" She grabs her laptop and looks up her calendar. "I don't have anything a week out, but I have an opening at nine a.m. on Monday two weeks out. Does that work?"

"Yes."

Dr. Nash gets up and walks to the door. As she opens it, her usual smile is on her face, and she says her usual end-of-session statement. "Take care of yourself, keep taking your meds correctly, and keep journaling your thoughts and feelings."

"Okay, I will," I say. I do none of these things.

CHAPTER 6:

I wake up groggy. Another night of restless sleep. I look at my phone and see that it's almost nine a.m. I look around my bedroom. It's a complete mess. I have a collection of water cups scattered around the room. Clothes overflow the laundry basket. The trashcans in the bedroom and bathroom are filled to the brim. It's an immediate demotivator to start a day. I know this, yet I still don't keep my place tidy. I have no reason to keep it clean. No one else comes here except Susan, showing up and looking past the doorway, judging me.

I stumble out of bed to the bathroom to brush my teeth and notice a pink ring forming around the toilet bowl. I look in the mirror at myself with cloudy eyes. "Today is the day that you will take care of all this mess. You can do it."

I spit out the toothpaste, and with that, the uncontrollable flow of judgments start to raid my morning. *Why can't you get it together? Your life is not that hard.*

I stumble to the kitchen. I need coffee like I need air. I can't get it into my system fast enough. I grab it as soon as it's ready and walk back to my art studio. A single bed for Sienna fits into the corner of the room.

I sit on the bed. This is the only room that's organized. I lie down and grab the throw folded at the bottom, hugging it to myself. Burying my face in it, I inhale. I can still detect the light smell of Sienna. My heart quivers, and my eyes burn with tears. My mind blanks. I let the tears flow until they stop.

Time to get my day going and start my work. I move like a force is holding me back. I decide to put on some real clothes for a change; perhaps that will inspire something.

As I grab a sweatshirt and jeans from my closet, I ponder the drab redundancy of my life. Nothing to invoke my creativity or bring me happiness. Perhaps Arin was onto something.

I need a change, to mix things up. Something that I don't expect or despise. Day-to-day routine is a Groundhog Day of insanity with no hope of change. I guess that's why I wasn't cut out for marriage or family life where routine is essential. Only I seem to have created the redundancy without the family. Life's practical joke. I thought I could get away. Joke's on me.

The boxed butterfly mocks me from my easel, where I'd put it after I picked it up off the floor. I transfer it to my pin-up board and grab a blank canvas. I have no desire to work. I could draw my future, the future that I want to happen, instead of this life. But it's what I can't control that strikes me deeply. I can't transport myself back in time and change what I did. I can't change that my ex-husband, Sienna's father, loathes my existence, and that Sienna is no longer here.

I suddenly hear the text alert on my phone. It's Arin.
Good morning Em, I hope ur feeling better. I dreamt that I paid for your trip to Asheville. So real. It was a sign. Book a cabin in Asheville or that lake for at least a month, send me the payment info. Do it now! It's a gift. Learn how to accept a gift.

I can't believe Arin. Always wanting to be the savior, dammit. Is she feeling guilty? I hate that she can be forgiven by paying for extravagant things. Asking her what she was saying to Mariam about Sienna now feels inappropriate. I shake it off. *She gets to live the life she wants with no financial barriers. I'll use her money to fund my trip.*

As quickly as the annoyance entered, relief and a bit of excitement take over. An uncontrollable smile spreads over my face. My imagination takes over as I think about the opportunity, the reprieve from the mundane, something else along my path. I need it. I crave it like a creek needs water.

I text Arin:
Okay, you got me. I accept. Thank you. You totally didn't have to do this.

She texts back right away:
The more I think about it, the more I know this is the right decision.

If Arin feels guilty for what she said about me, then I'll at least get something good out of it. I grab my laptop and open it on my small desk so I can google vacation rentals. I go through several cabins; nothing grabs my attention. *As if I've earned the right to be particular*, I scoff to myself. *I'm channeling Arin's selective energy*.

Realizing that, if I had my way, I'd choose a cabin that's old, something with character, to feed my need for nostalgia. Something strange and different, perhaps retro. I can pretend to be someone else from a different time, someone other than me.

I look at the time in the corner of the screen, and two hours have passed. I'm relieved. It was a couple of hours' break from torturing myself about the reality of the moment. My body feels a sense of alleviation. There is peace. A double relief too. It's a distraction from my lack of productivity and a hell of a reason to procrastinate. I'll start painting when I'm at the cabin.

I think about the night before with the art collectors. Pain stabs my heart and expels anxiety through it. Embarrassment circulates through my body. Another shameful story to add to my collection. It stings. But just like one moment to the next can invite a new piece of information, I remember what Mariam and George said about the lake near Asheville. *What was the name of that lake?*

Recharged, I google lakes near Asheville, and there it is. A lake in the shape of an intersection, two roads crossing—Lake Lure. I search through cabin after cabin, but the mood, setting, or something else is off-putting—the house isn't unique enough, too big or too small, dated, or odd floorplan. Time for a break.

I stretch my arms and tilt my head back. I look back at the computer screen as my email dings. And there in my inbox awaits an email with a photo of a cabin attached to it. *Google Analytics. Now, that's some scary shit.*

The cabin is a 1940s home that has been renovated. It has a farmhouse, rustic look. Decor is minimalistic. Two bedrooms and one bath, lakefront with a dock, and two kayaks. The pictures of the cabin jump out at me as if it were saying, "Em, this is your home; come and live in me." *If I had the money, I would buy this place.*

Perhaps the sad energy that I carry with me will be transformed, metamorphosized into happiness—a happy ending. Isn't that what we're taught? Nothing can end badly, we will save the day, eventually—just have faith to make it through.

Arin pays for the cabin and adds an extra thousand dollars for spending money and guilt. It's a done deal. With that, Lake Lure will be my home for one month.

CHAPTER 7:

One day to go until I leave for my trip. I wake up feeling excited to start the day for the first time in a while. There is a purpose, a distraction, something I can look forward to. Had I known that booking a trip to a cabin would be an immediate antidepressant, I would have asked Arin for the money a long time ago.

I rise out of bed, and instead of staring at the mess around my place, I start to clean it. One by one, I stack cups and take them to the sink. I pick up my clothes, sort and wash them. I load the dishwasher and wash the big pots by hand. I grab my speaker, sync the Bluetooth to my phone, and listen to an old playlist.

I empty the trash, and when I come back inside, I check my phone and see that I just missed a call from Chastain. She and I have been friends since we were twelve. There have been a few hiccups when we weren't close—different moves to different schools, separate colleges, marriages—where life took us away from each other. Losing touch is always forgiven, and we fall right back into our friendship as if six or two or however many years hadn't passed. Even though we come from different racial backgrounds, me White and her Black, our lives still connect in a seamless way.

Perhaps our connection is through the lack of mothering we both felt. Our shared life challenges united us in ways we never spoke about. Our mothers were two human beings with only one thing in common: they weren't there when we needed them.

Chastain did well for herself. I knew she would from the time we were kids. Her grades were better than mine, and she was more invested in school. I was partying; she was studying. I was too immature and reckless to care about growing up. She dealt with her life by beating the odds, driven to be the opposite of her mom. She was steadfast and focused on those around her who were successful, mirroring them as her mentors, her guides. Perhaps it's her innate ability to read other people, paying homage to subtle gestures that most people wouldn't notice. Or maybe it's her uncanny memory that won't let her forget any interaction that stamped her mind. Things she would rather not remember.

I get a notice of a text from her.

Hey Em, just checking in. How are you, my lady?

Good, I'm going to the mountains tomorrow. How are you?

What! Are you serious? Who are you going with?

By myself, to get work done. No creativity flowing here.

Wow, call me when you can, I want to know the details.

After cleaning the bathroom, I call Chastain. "Hey, Chas, how are you?"

With relief in her voice, Chastain says, "I'm good. So you're leaving tomorrow?"

"Yes, I'm just cleaning up the place, and tomorrow I plan to pack and head out."

"Em, you sound good."

"I'm, actually...good."

"How long are you going for?"

"That's the best part! A month! Arin is paying for the whole trip; it was her idea, actually."

"Oh, good ol' loaded Arin. I mean...she has the money, why not?"

"Yeah, I think she felt guilty about the other night. I mean, I probably feel worse than she does. I made a fool of myself."

"What happened?"

"I walked in on her talking about Sienna behind my back. To an art collector, of all people."

Chastain's voice lowers. "Oh, um... What was she saying?"

"I don't know; that's the thing. Probably telling her my sad story so the lady would feel sorry for me and buy my art. She always sells art by grabbing people's hearts. I don't approve of her doing that when it's about me. It's so insensitive."

Thinking about it makes me feel horrible and sad again. I want to forget about it. I want to forget how people look at me like they feel sorry for me.

"Maybe she wasn't saying anything bad. Maybe she was just concerned about you."

The emotions start to rise again, and I feel invalidated. "Oh, Chas, not you too. I already talked to Dr. Nash about it. No one seems to understand why it's upsetting to me. And Arin also lied to me about talking about Sienna. I forgot to mention that."

Chastain takes a deep breath. "I get it, Em. At least Arin felt bad and paid for your trip. That's amazing. Listen, I want you to call me when you get there, and please send me the address before you leave."

"Okay, Mother. You know, you need to relax a little."

"Whatever. Listen, be super careful, and if you hear banjos, get the hell out of Dodge. I don't understand how you can go to a cabin in the mountains by yourself. You know you're asking for a *Scream 8* situation. Courteney Cox is getting too old for this shit, I'm tellin' you."

We both laugh. "Well, I can't focus enough to finish my pieces for the Metamorphosis exhibit. I need a change of scenery."

"Right. Just stay in touch, please, Em. Don't forget to send me the address."

We hang up.

Chastain always makes me feel so much lighter. Her laughter soothes me and gives me something else to think about.

I spend the rest of the day cleaning up my apartment. Remembering bits and pieces of our conversation, I occasionally laugh to myself. If only the feeling could last longer, it would be the all-encompassing thread of emotion throughout my day. I keep going until the apartment is spotless. I'm exhausted. I find beans and rice in the freezer and half an avocado in the fridge. That's dinner.

CHAPTER 8:

I'm on the road. It's three in the afternoon, and I need to get there before the sun goes down. Driving at night in the mountains isn't smart, especially when I don't know where I'm going. It takes three hours to get to Lake Lure from Atlanta, so I should have plenty of time.

An hour has passed, and the feeling of driving forward is somehow comforting. I'm moving forward, but my mind still wants to go backward. I think about Kyle. I haven't talked to him in so long. I remember when we first met.

Kyle was not my type at all, the handsome Caucasian all-American guy. He was taller with a strong, athletic build. He came from a good family and did what he was supposed to do in life. I was used to dating the troubled kind. Guys who had divorced parents, were rebellious, and liked to party too much. We were attending Georgia State University when we met for the second time.

My roommate, Jena, a redhead, talked me into taking Speech instead of a foreign language, which seemed like an easier option at the time. Having serious anxiety during public speaking, Jena and I both took two shots of vodka before we went into class on the morning of our first informative speech. We giggled all the way to class over our secret, a one-up on everyone else, uniting us in an alliance that created a pseudo-confidence for our performances. It worked. We both nailed our speeches.

I gave mine on organic farming. I had interviewed my grandfather on the subject. Kyle was sitting in the front, and I noticed his deep stare about halfway through my talk. Even though he wasn't my type, something about him made me blush. He wasn't just listening to my speech with a slight smile on his face; he was watching me like he gave a damn about organic farming.

Once I collapsed in relief in my seat, Jena said, "Holy shit! Did you notice front row hottie staring at you?"

I replied with an innocent smile, "I have no idea what you're talking about."

Having successfully given our speeches without dying from a panic attack, we both strutted out of class. I felt a tap on my shoulder from behind, and I turned to find Kyle had caught up to us.

He said, "You know we know each other, right?"

Jena started to laugh from the awkwardness of the moment, then stopped herself. I couldn't stop myself from smiling too. "Um....no. How do we know each other?"

When I looked at him a bit closer, I saw a resemblance to a young boy I used to know. "Wait... No way! Kyle Smith from third grade?"

"That's me."

The transition from talking to someone to sharing a first kiss, in my experience, can be executed well, or it can be a complete and utter disaster. When it was a disaster, you either followed through with the kiss to avoid making the person feel bad, or you flat out refused it.

Kyle invited me to hang out with his roommate, and I brought Jena along. Jena and Kyle's roommate, Matt, a brown-haired man, hit it off right away. Kyle and I seemed to be in our own world. Kyle's focus was on me, and it excited me. When the time came for our first kiss, there was no awkwardness about it.

Jena and Matt were chatting on the back porch, smoking cigarettes.

We were alone, and it was getting late. We were sitting on his living room couch, and I had a drink in my hand. He grabbed it and set it on the table beside the couch, then pushed my knees apart and kneeled in front of me. He looked at me for a moment without saying anything. My dress hiked up as he came in for the kiss, moving his body forward between my legs as I leaned into him. Our bodies wanted each other first, then our minds. Our lips collided, and the passion ignited. The intensity of the contact synergized the kiss. It was the best first kiss I'd ever had.

I had Sienna one year later, and we were married six months after her birth. We'd made a pact to finish college, and we did. Kyle was promised a high-up position at his grandfather's company with the hopes of one day taking over the business. Kyle and I were great together until we had Sienna; then everything changed.

Our marriage now seems surreal, like it was another me. So far from who I am now. A square peg in a round hole was how I'd felt, being married. I wasn't me, and I was miserable. Kyle was the opposite; he had exactly what he wanted. A marriage and a life like every other family. I tried to play the part, but I wanted my performance to end. End of story—now let's get on with real life. Only real life wasn't all that great either. I got it wrong, although I was true to myself. I thought my story would be happy, finally.

Sienna stayed with Kyle, and Kyle remarried. My performance as a mother ended, and I assumed my role as a sideline mother—second rate, meaning shit rate. My responsibility, originally so great and important, fell away, and I lost all rights to the role. It's either all or nothing. You can't just do it sometimes. When you're a mother, you're everything. You're the center of the household universe. If you can't get the help you need from your partner, then it's your own problem. The household is your domain by default. How you manage the domain is up to you.

Kyle didn't want anything to do with Sienna at first. It was all me. I felt helpless, secluded, alone. My friends were fulfilling their dreams, traveling, getting higher degrees, and living out their twenties in foolishness, with no real consequences for their single lives, while my life got serious quickly.

I wasn't prepared. I didn't know that I couldn't do it all. I was up in the middle of the night, feeding her and then putting her back to sleep. Repeat. I didn't look forward to the following day because it was just taking care of a baby all on my own with no end in sight. Fearing that I might do something wrong, not wanting to be separated from her, yet miserable being chained to her.

My dream was to be an artist, and Kyle made enough to support a good life, but art wasn't my real profession. My role was full-time mother instead. Kyle called art my hobby. And because he made enough money, my job was to take care of the household and the baby. Kyle's job was to take care of the money. There. We had our roles. Do what you're supposed to do, and that's that. Kyle finally started stepping up when he realized there were times that I couldn't get out of bed.

I look down at my gas gauge and realize I'm running low. Shit. Exits are now few and far between. I pass trees and trees and more trees. Every second feels like a minute, and every minute feels like an hour. I check my gas gauge again, then the time—five minutes, then ten. This doesn't feel right. How is it possible that I need gas on the longest stretch of I-85N without an exit? Did I blink or zone out and miss my exit? Did I turn off onto some other highway by mistake? I worry that my memories overcame my present so much that I'd lost track of where I am.

My head starts to tingle, and the prickly hairs on my body stand up. Pounding. My heart is pounding. My face goes numb, and the reality of the situation, like life is trying to teach me something, overwhelms me. Pay attention. Be aware, or things like this can happen. I feel helpless and alone and stupid. No one I know is available to come get me. I'm already an hour and a half outside of Atlanta. The gas gauge is past the lowest line. My car will stop any moment now. My anxiety is at a height with disgust filling my gut, and vomit rising to my throat. Vision narrowing and getting smaller. Ears becoming muffled, holding my breath underwater. The opposite reaction to flight or fight, my senses shutting down, altered. Pain shoots up the left side of my neck, a force pushing me down. *Breathe...breathe...breathe.*

Should I stop on the side of the road? No. What if I can't get the car to start again? There's no one on the road. I'm somewhere, but I'm nowhere. Shit. Shit. Shit. Wait, I see something up ahead. It's a sign. The sign reads *Texaco* and some other gas stations, but will I make it? Did my car just jerk a little? Come on, come on car! I won't ever do this to you again, if only you can make it to the gas station.

I make it to the gas station. My heart slows, and my breath calms. I sit there for a minute to gather myself. There's one other car parked by another gas pump. Pop the lever to open the gas tank, press 87 grade, grab the nozzle, and fill her up.

I stare at the dollars sprinting upward, hear the gurgling sound as the gas streams into the tank. I've never been so ecstatic to have the sweet chemical smell of refined petroleum seeping into my nostrils. A feeling of exhaustion overtakes me. Too much stress on the nervous system has my mind muted.

I stare off. The gas station is a lone business surrounded by trees. Two older cars are parked at the convenience store. Trash scattered throughout the parking lot hangs out, then scuttles along as a breeze passes. Another battered car on the far edge of the parking area appears abandoned and has taken root. Cracks in the concrete harbor small patches of grass near the untraveled edges of the parking lot.

I catch movement from the corner of my eye—the other car parked at the pump diagonal to mine. A person busily opening car doors and shutting them, cleaning out the car, perhaps.

I glance at the dollar meter and then back at the other car to see a woman staring at me. Pang through my heart, fear, my anxiety back in full gear. I flash a smile. My reactive response to covering up uneasiness. I look down, but there's an odd recognition that pulls my eyes back up to face the woman again. I thought she looked Asian, like Mei. But when I look back up, she's placing the nozzle back and getting in her car. I can't see her face the way she's turned. She starts her car. She pulls forward, slows, turns, and passes by me, looking me dead in the eye. I stare, trying to figure out if it truly is Mei, only to discover this woman is not at all like Mei, but instead she has large brown eyes and brown hair.

What? I shake it off. I need to relax. I'm just driving to a cabin three hours from Atlanta; it's not that tough. I place the nozzle back, finish payment, and get in my car but pause before putting the key in the ignition. *The only bad thing that can happen is all in my head.* Mei gets tucked back into a corner of my mind where I can safely avoid her. I turn up the music on my playlist and block out the conflict in my head to focus on something real. *Simon and Garfunkel are real.* The tunes distract and deflect. I start the car and drive off. I'm on my way to the cabin, and I won't let my fears turn me back.

CHAPTER 9:

The sky dumps water on my car just as I'm getting off the exit for Lake Lure. It's as if Mother Nature timed it. The clouds have made it darker than usual during this time of day, and the constant pounding of rain makes it impossible to see anything farther than three feet in front of me. It reminds me of going through car washes at gas stations with my mom. I loved to watch how the automatic dispenser would squirt soap all over the car and then the big brush would roll over us, washing the dirt away. My mom would have a look of excitement as she watched me, as if we were at an amusement park, buckled in for a scary ride. We'd pull out of the car wash after the job was done, the windshield wipers sloshing off the leftover water.

The rain cascades off my car as I exit the highway and come to a stop sign on a two-lane road. I can only go left or right. It's dark as night. Between the swishing of buckets of water, I see a giant cross with a sign that reads *Jesus is Coming* in front of me. I make a left turn as instructed by the GPS.

The rain is pounding on the car. It's all I can focus on. I glance down at the GPS. Another forty-three minutes left to go. I breathe out my frustration at the speedometer showing thirteen miles per hour. The road has no streetlights, and my car is the only one in sight. I pass what looks like a small town with a gas station, a Subway, and a dollar store at the corner and make a careful turn onto another street.

The darkness ignites a vulnerability within me. My senses are heightened. The steadfast thudding of rain gets louder, the swishing of the windshield wipers back and forth, back and forth. The headlights barely illuminate dark outlines of trees between swishes.

I'm pulled into a memory, a regression in time. A Scrooge scenario, the ghost of Christmas past summoned from within.

I'm lost, trying to find Sienna's soccer game. Kyle confused the game location with next week's game. I've spent thirty minutes searching for a familiar face, going to field after field. Finally, I call Kyle. "Hey, did you say that Sienna is playing on field two?"

"Yes, field two."

"Okay, well I'm looking at field two, and it's two completely different teams. Sienna's team is nowhere to be found."

"I don't know what to tell you."

"Well, Kyle, did you give me the right location?"

Kyle's voice becomes muffled. "Laura, what's the name of this soccer field? Emily says she can't find it."

I overhear Laura's sarcastic reply. "Really? I'm shocked. It's Glenwood Soccer Park in Decatur."

Kyle repeats the location. Tears of frustration come to my eyes. "Kyle, I'm at the UFA soccer field in Norcross. Why did you tell me to go to UFA? Now, I'm going to miss at least half her game. She's not going to forgive me for that."

Kyle spits out, "Oh, you're something else. You're going to blame me for your absence in Sienna's life. What next? We take her to practices, we pay for everything she does, and what do you do? You barely make an effort to show up. All you have to do is show up."

Too angry to speak, I remain silent. No way to respond, no excuse to be given. The phone call ends, and the shame begins. This isn't the first time a wrong place has been given to me, or a mess-up with directions on my part, or something else that keeps me from getting out of bed and facing my beautiful

Sienna. Sometimes it hurts too much to see Sienna happy and blissful, living her life without me.

Kyle used to make excuses for me when I couldn't make it. *Your mom isn't feeling well.* But one occasion adds up to many, and when many add up, something else evolves. Sienna stopped expecting my calls, and the visits felt forced when she came to stay at my place. She'd rather go to a friend's house.

Kyle started telling me that she had other things to do, like soccer tournaments or sleepovers. "You don't want her to miss out on this, right, Emily?" Every other weekend became every three weeks, then once a month.

Showing my face to a team of soccer parents who don't recognize I'm Sienna's mother feels like punishment. I'm relegated to the farthest corner of the bleachers, eye contact forbidden and awkward. Keep to yourself. Keep your distance. Speak only when spoken to. They scream Sienna's name when she makes a goal, hug her after the games, plan playdates, and coordinate carpool for practices. I never know who these people are who associate with dear Sienna. Accepting my fate, I maintain my position, this role of the sideline mother.

I arrive to the game at halftime. As I'm walking to the field, I smell hot dogs and popcorn and hear the faint screams of parents and whistles blowing from other soccer games. Younger siblings are doing cartwheels, and toddlers are being herded away from the sidelines.

I find the right field and avoid the areas where all the parents from the team are gathering. I spot Kyle and Laura talking with some other family. Skirting past them unnoticed, I walk over to let Sienna know that I'm there. Getting as close to the team as possible, I make eye contact with her. I smile and wave. As if I'm invisible, Sienna doesn't wave back. I wave again and yell out Sienna's name. She looks right through me as if I'm not there. There's no change in her expression, just a neutral look, then she turns back to her teammate.

I'm yanked out of my memory by a knock at the window. My car is stopped, and I'm sitting in an old Baptist church parking lot. My windshield wipers are still going, my lights are on, and I'm sitting there staring at the woods in front of me. The car isn't in park, but I have my foot on the brake, and the car is inching forward.

I jump from the knock, causing my foot to come off the brake, and the car jolts forward. I slam on the brake, and the car jerks to a stop.

It's a police officer. He has pale skin and large brown eyes that appear to pop out of his face. Out of sorts, I lower my window. The rain streams off the brim of his hat. With a southern drawl, the officer asks, "Ma'am, are you all right?"

"Uh, yes, I'm fine. Sorry, I must have gotten sidetracked."

"Ma'am, do me a favor and put your car in park." I blush and do as I'm told.

"Are you under the influence of any drugs or alcohol?"

"No, sir. I was just really scared with the rain coming down."

"Pastor Jamieson over there saw you in the parking lot." He points to a house beside the church. The front porch light is on, and I notice a man standing there looking at us.

"He's never seen your car before and wanted to make certain everything was okay. He's had some trouble in the past with kids up to no good. Where ya headed?"

"Um, Lake Lure, to a cabin. I can give you the address if you want."

I search my email to find the reservation and show the officer. "Look, I'm so sorry about this. Sometimes I get nervous when I'm driving in the rain."

The officer shines his flashlight on the phone, reads the reservation. "You're at the old Howard place? I didn't realize they were renting it out." He stares at the phone for a second, then his tone changes. "What company is renting it?"

I scroll down on my phone. "There, Lake Lure Rental Company."

The police officer pauses, face unreadable.

I'm getting nervous now. "Is there a problem with the rental? I can show you the receipt of payment if you still don't believe me."

The officer responds, "I...believe you. There's just...I don't know." He stares off again, then looks back at me. "I'm gonna let you go now, but please make sure you're paying attention to the road."

"Okay, Officer, I will. Thank you so much."

"Drive safely." The officer looks toward his patrol car, then walks up to the pastor's house instead.

I check the GPS on my phone to figure out which way I need to go. After a last look at the officer and the pastor talking on the porch, I turn around to head out. They just watch as I leave the parking lot.

My GPS says thirty-three more minutes. I still drive slowly. The rain has let up a little, but not enough to help with visibility. I can't make out much in front of me but darkness and trees. The road seems to be going straight, no mountainous twists and turns to curve around.

After about five minutes, the rain stops just as abruptly as it started. I can see more clearly. There are high banks on the left side of the road and what looks like a river on the right. I figure I must be in the foothills of the mountains I'm heading to. The relief of being able to see better relaxes me. Easing my hold on the steering wheel, I notice the ache in my fingers from gripping it. My shoulders hurt from being so tense, and a slight strain travels down the left side of my neck. I turn my head from side to side and roll my shoulders back to release the tension.

Breaking the uncanny silence, I say out loud to no one, "Okay, time to get some music on, get some new energy flowing through here. Let's see whatcha got."

I turn on the radio and fumble through staticky stations, settling on one that comes in clearly. "Praise Jesus when he arrives.

You will go to hell if you don't accept the Lord as your savior. He will cast you down, and you will burn in hell, and he will take all your family and neighbors that don't accept the Lord Jesus…"

I recite with a southern accent, "Jesus…lord Jesus, he who takes thy lord in vain will burn like a hot dog on a stick over a campfire."

I laugh, trying to banish the feeling of fear in my gut. "Okay, not what I'm going for." Skipping through channels of country, gospel, and more church sermons, I finally land on an oldies station. The song playing is *People are Strange* by The Doors. Music that certainly captures the moment. "No freaking way."

I turn up the volume and start singing along. I'm in the middle of the second round of the chorus when I'm blinded by headlights from behind me. The car slows, moves as though it's going to pass me, but then seems to settle in behind me. "Okay, mister, go ahead and pass me. I'm going like three miles per hour."

I start to slow a little more so the car will pass, but it doesn't. After about five minutes, it finally goes around me. The car slows beside me, and I look over. The driver is a younger-looking male with shaggy blond hair. He stares at me with a wicked smile, then makes the two-fingers-to-eyes gesture that means *I'm watching you.*

"What the fuck?" I shout. He speeds up, moves back into the lane in front of me, and keeps going. I stop the car and watch until I can no longer see his taillights. Shaken, my body shivers as if to rid the experience from my consciousness.

I look at the directions on my phone, and I'm thirteen minutes away from the cabin. *Oh, thank God.* This shit drive needs to end with a bottle of good red wine. Fortunately, I'd stopped by the store before hitting the road and wiped them out of my favorite pinot noir. A glass couldn't come quick enough.

With only a few twists and turns, the last few miles to the cabin are uneventful. Except for the sharp turn into the driveway. *The directions could have said something about that*, I think. While inching down the steep driveway, I see the clearing and the lake in front of me as if I'm parking at a drive-in theater and the moonlit lake is the opening scene. I stop and turn off the car for its well-deserved night's rest.

I can see sparkles reflecting off the water, lights from nearby docks. The house is in a cove. It overlooks the lake with the dock as the backyard. The rain clouds made their point, overstayed their welcome, and exited to leave behind a clear night in hopes of an exceptional day to follow. The moonlight from above reflects a gateway to the open water. The view is stunning and eerie at the same time. The night creatures debut their spring symphony, playing their hearts out, background music to the scene. I'm stunned by its brilliance and the uneasiness that has taken root in my stomach.

I could go back to Atlanta, to the sameness of the days and routine that I can expect. Here, I'm vulnerable to nature, to loneliness, to this new town, as I try to pull together a successful art show or face more failure. The possibilities are unknown yet exhilarating. I hadn't considered how important this trip was until now, how purposeful and proactive it feels. Routinely being subjected to judgment, I sense a way to recapture life, fully participate in it, as a result of this gesture, this decision.

Tears pour from my eyes, this time from joy rather than sadness. To take hold of the life that has been slipping through my fingers, I enter the rental at Lake Lure, hoping to change the course of my path.

CHAPTER 10:

I awake to what I figure is the middle of the night in a bed that's not mine. The mattress has adjusted to my form. I feel paralyzed, unable to move. It's still dark outside.

I was dreaming about the drive to the rental. It felt real. I kept making wrong turns, even though I was following the GPS. I kept ending up on streets where I didn't want to be. Locals were walking along the sides of the streets, staring at me as if they knew I didn't belong. I kept turning down road after road, making the same mistake again and again. Most of the roads were dirt or gravel, and it was dark. My headlights shone on the backs of people's heads, and they turned and stared. I couldn't find the right direction, no matter how many times I looked at my GPS. The car wouldn't turn the right way, just went down roads that led nowhere with no purpose.

Feeling the beginnings of a dull headache, I turn on the lamp on the bedside table and notice a red wineglass, a quarter full, sitting next to a bottle of unopened water. I twist the cap off the water and drink half of the bottle, the quenching of thirst signaling dehydration that I'd been unaware of. I look at the time on my phone. It's three in the morning, and I missed a text from Chas. I text Chas back that I made it, and everything is good.

Go back to sleep, I think. A few minutes later I drift into a deep slumber.

CHAPTER 11:

It's late morning when I wake up. I'm still dressed in my clothes from the night before. I don't remember falling asleep or how I got to bed. I'm struggling to remember where I am. My last memory was of looking at the lake.

I check my phone, and it's after ten. My blurry eyes try to focus with the brightness all around. The bed is covered in pure white linens. There are two bedside tables with matching lamps, a dresser, and large windows with curtains drawn on both sides. I sit up and turn to stand. My legs feel tired, like I've been running all night. I head out of the bedroom, and I'm welcomed by the panoramic view of the lake. A sight that brings me instant joy.

The cabin is even better than I thought. The windows at the back of the house are huge, giving an all-encompassing view of the lake. The two bedrooms are at the front of the house with the bathroom in the middle. A short hallway enters an open floorplan with the living room to the right, a sliding glass door straight ahead that connects to the screened-in porch. The kitchen to the left is separated from the living room by stairs that lead to the basement. The porch takes up the whole back side of the house, with a hundred-and-eighty-degree view of the lake. Impressive.

I grab a throw from the couch, wrap it around me, and walk out to the porch. The slight chill in the air bites my skin. I look out onto the lake and feel a sense of clarity. This was the right decision. Already energized, I feel a tingling sensation all over my body, and it's not the chill in the air. It's something I haven't felt in a long time. Appreciation for where I'm at right now—the moment is okay. It's not terrible. In fact, it's welcome. This place has its own life force. The vibrations are intense. I want to humble myself before its authority. This place on Lake Lure could capture me, and I'm smitten by its essence, by the timelessness.

The sun has risen just above the trees and is shining on the lake. The cove has several docks, but the one at this house is separated in its own mini cove, a little offset from the rest. The lake is bustling, full of people on kayaks and SUPs. One of the SUPs has a Scottie dog sitting on the front, barking at the water while its owner paddles through the cove.

Across the water on the other side, two teenage girls lie on a dock looking at their phones. I have a clear view of the open water outside the main cove, and boats speed past.

I go back to the house and look for coffee. There's a Keurig. *Yes, instant gratification.* I put in a pod, and I'm drinking coffee within two minutes. I look around the kitchen. The window above the sink looks out to the side of the house. A weathered piece of wooden artwork that reads *Life is Better at the Lake* is hanging above the window. The bottle of red is still on the dining room table. I'm relieved that I only drank a glass instead of the whole bottle. My relief is short-lived when I pass by the trash can and see the empty bottle inside. *Shit. Perhaps that's the reason I can't remember last night.*

I put the cold groceries into the refrigerator the night before, but everything else is still in the bags on the counter. On the living room couch, all my art supplies are piled up. Spooked from the drive, I'd grabbed everything as fast as I could from the car and set them down wherever there was room.

I begin to arrange my supplies on the built-in console table that backs up to the basement stairs. The house might be in total disarray, but my art supplies are never out of order. I organize the acrylic paints and set them in a row. I grab all the paintbrushes and put them in the holder. The canvases I set in front of the table on the floor, leaning them up against one another. I arrange the alcohol markers in another canister, along with the drawing utensils, then set the charcoal beside it. Pleased with the arrangement, I go back to the bedroom and throw on comfy pants and a sweatshirt. The curtains are closed, so I open them to let in the natural light.

I walk back to the porch and smell the air—crisp and fresh. The mountains provide a backdrop to the lake and trees. I lie down on the outdoor couch and see remnants of the 1940s version of this home. They kept the old to build character—just slapped some paint on it. Replaced or updated the utilitarian, like the kitchen, flooring, and bathrooms, but to accentuate the style that has expired. Re-stained old trim around doorways and windows, repurposed and used structures in other places, and kept faucets that were in good condition. I'm enthralled with every detail of this house. The combination of new and old is synergistic.

What really makes this cabin brilliant is the view. With one look, it takes my breath and numbs my mind to where I can only focus on its striking entirety. It's the strength of the mountains, the dignity of the trees, and the restorative powers of the water that I marvel at, all looking their best. With a blink, I can capture its eminence and vivacity. *Why don't I live here, where life seems so buoyant? Perhaps a getaway shack along the water might reset my stagnant mind and open a fortress of creativity. I might feel whole again.*

As I lie there, the hours fly by. I feel as though I'm living in the forties. My entertainment is my vista, the interaction between people and the activities ranging from floating platforms to splashing and distant screams. Gusts of wind blow my hair, chill my skin, and send my nose subtle floral scents. Butterflies fly past, while ducks chill on docks—things that are alive. I'm alive. I've never been so alive until now.

And then…a knock on the door disrupts my afternoon show. *Who's here?*

CHAPTER 12:

I'm startled from the knock and pop up off the couch. I can't see from the porch who's at the front door, so I go back inside. When I open the door, I see a tall White man with gray hair. He has on a white button-down shirt with black slacks and nice shoes. He's holding a basket. I meet his gaze with a questioning smile.

The man responds with a Carolina drawl. "Hi, miss. We saw you moving in some stuff last night, and my wife, Carol, and I wanted to welcome you to the lake. Sorry Carol couldn't make it. She's playing bridge with some friends. We didn't want to miss you like last time. We live next door, over to the right." He points to the side of his house.

Last time? I realize what must have happened. "I'm sorry, I didn't catch your name."

The man chuckles. "I'm Tom, Tom West."

"Hi, Tom. Nice to meet you. I'm Emily. I'm not the owner of this house. I'm just renting it for a month."

Tom stands there with a confused look on his face for a minute. "Well, it's been a while since we saw her, and it was far away. I'm sorry to bother you. I'll let Carol know our mistake. Please take this basket, or else I won't hear the end of it from my wife. It's local honey, a bottle of wine from the winery in Chimney Rock, and a Welcome to Lake Lure dish towel. Carol special orders the towels."

I sense a warmth from this man. "Well, I wouldn't want your wife to get mad, so I'll take these lovely gifts. I don't deserve them, but thank you."

"So...you're staying for a month?"

"Yes."

"Well, right now is the perfect time to come. The weather is nice for kayaking, and the butterflies are out. Our granddaughter, Lily, loves to count them. Last year she counted thirty-six butterflies in one day."

"That's great."

"Well, I hope you enjoy the lake. Did you say you're here all by yourself?"

"Um, yes, that's right."

"Well, you're a brave woman. Carol would never travel alone like that."

"I don't feel so alone. I've got my sketchpad and the view of the lake. I'm perfectly fine."

"Ah, you're an artist? Carol was an art teacher before she retired. She still paints. You'd like my wife. You should meet her for tea or coffee. You can compare art notes or something, and you won't feel so alone."

"Well, I don't really feel so alone," I repeat, "but I'd be happy to meet Carol." That's a lie. In my experience, older women ask personal questions, and they're all about your family life. I'm not in the mood to be judged.

"Great. I'll let Carol know we have an artist staying beside us. She'll be thrilled.

We're right next door, so holler if you need us."

I need to find a way out of this. "Thank you so much again. I do have a question. Can you recommend any good restaurants around here?"

"Well, there's an Italian place by the lake's beach access. They have great pizza. If you like the bottle of wine we gave you, go to Chimney Rock and taste more of their wines. You'll enjoy the view on a nice day."

"Well...I might just do that. Thank you, Tom. Have a good day, and tell Carol I said thank you."

Tom smiles. "You can tell her yourself."

"Oh, right. Looking forward to it." Tom waves and walks off.

I close the door and look at the basket. I wish I was the real owner of the house. I sit down on the couch and realize for the first time in a long time I'm happy. *A vacation, a reprieve from reality... Arin is right.*

The urge to draw is beckoning me. Barefoot still, I walk over to my art supplies, grab my sketchbook, and plop down on the outdoor couch. I sketch an image of an elegant woman sitting on a porch swing looking out over a lake. A couple of effortless hours go by, and I come to a stopping point. The neighbor's gift has been calling my name. *I wonder how a bottle of North Carolina wine might taste.*

CHAPTER 13:

I uncork the bottle of wine that is said to be harvested from this area. I pour it in my glass and swish it around. As I sip, I envision it as a cultivation of this place, this piece of earth, flooding into my body. The enriched juice numbs my insides and makes its way up to dull my mind. I close my eyes, and I'm lost in my head and in the moment.

Music. My earbuds are nestled inside my ears, and I feel the song run through my veins. It's Sam Smith's remake of *I Feel Love* by Donna Summer. Before my mind catches on, I'm moving to it. Turn up the volume, and I'm moving my arms to one instrument and rhythm, my hips to another. No set choreography, no mind directing what's next, just the free flow of body to the music, trusting the euphony and that my body will follow it. Wine loosens my inhibitions and advances my ability to feel it rather than hear it. The porch is my dance floor. The experience is in between the beat and the rhythm, riding the tune through waves as my body matches it. Eyes closed, swaying, moving in a way that parallels the song. Something arises from within. Another feeling or intelligence. It's something that comes along with action. A reaction to this blend of body and rhythm. Perhaps its spirit, soul, or something larger than me. This goes on for a while.

My eyes open; I'm not sure why. Natural daylight hits, and I'm blinded by the brightness. The mountains, the trees, then the distant lake come into focus. Directing my gaze downward,

I see two men staring up at me from a fishing boat. One of the men jolts as he realizes I see their stares.

How long have they been there watching me? They turn away as if they were never looking. One discreetly smiles at his partner, and the other shakes his head and laughs. They float through the cove around the edges where fish hang, circulating farther away from my view.

An anxious pang hits. An awareness that my inner world could be viewed by others. I would prefer to be invisible. Inappropriate times of expression call for judged responses. Many times I want to be visible, yet no one sees me. Never the result lining up with the desire.

I'm reminded of so many other defenseless moments in my life, far too many to count. This one isn't bad in comparison to the rest. No single experience comes to mind, but a collage of them put into a flimsy trash bag, easily torn to spill out onto the street.

The sun starts to set. I can see its descent into the mountains, saying goodbye to another day. I fill up my glass with wine.

Then I grab my canvas and begin to paint.

CHAPTER 14:

I wake up early. It's still dark outside, one of the best times of the day. The sun ever so gently announces its presence. So polite in this gesture, the slow rise of light to meet me. A time of contemplation, a moment of reflection on what's to come. Prepare the day. I never seem to be able to wake at this most opportune time, always after it has passed.

My plan for this day is to eat, paint, and explore the town.

I look out onto the lake from the living room to a scene that calms my soul and tells me everything will be okay. But even in this setting, my gut tells me otherwise. The calmness, coffee, and sunlight creeping into day take me back in time.

Sienna was just born. Several friends and lots of family members came to the hospital to see her. Everyone was excited to meet her. I was shocked at how many people came. There wasn't a moment that Kyle and I were alone. It was unexpected—everything about the experience. The invasion of support, feeling like it was too much, yet in retrospect missing it at the times when there was no one.

As I relive this memory, I realize how important it was to see these people. The help from family was strong at the beginning and then trickled off as life continued and people had their own lives to attend. The love and support from people wore off, replaced by something new and unnerving.

Most people hate the hospital. I don't want to leave. It means I'll be taking care of this precious new human that I carried in my body, making sure she's cared for with the same precision but without a team of experts. The goal is impossible.

I read every book created about caring for a child. My trust in my ability to take care of another human being is low, yet determination for execution and a desire for perfection are very high.

Our parenting class at the hospital told us we should install our car seat base and then have it checked out by a police officer. Kyle placed the base in the car, and a police officer checked it out. Looking back, I realize Kyle was scared, just like me.

Walking out of the hospital with Sienna already snuggled in the seat feels like opening a door to some other world. Insecurity. We might do something wrong, and she might die. Or we might not feed her enough. Or what else could go wrong?

Kyle brings the car around to meet me with Sienna. The moments I sit waiting for Kyle feel like an eternity. She's asleep and could wake at any moment, and then what? No sound: Sienna sleeps. Kyle pulls forward. Snap...click. Sienna's car seat fits in the base. "Go slow, Kyle," I say.

"I know."

Being in a car feels new, like it's been ages since I'd been there, yet it's been only seventy-two hours. My world begins its descent into the unknown.

A sudden bad feeling shoots through my heart like I forgot something. I jerk my head to turn back to look at Sienna, but she's still snug and secure. At first glance, I think she might have stopped breathing. I stare longer and see her tiny lips purse out an exhale. Kyle, concerned, turns and asks me, "Is she okay?" I nod.

The vision of Sienna safe consoles me for the moment, but there are too many seconds to count in just one day. Too many different things that could occur. I realize now how powerless I feel as a mother. I want to do everything right, to have the healthiest and smartest baby possible. If I have all the information at my fingertips, then why can't I pull it off? Other women speak of a woman's intuition, but I think that feminine gene skipped me because I never feel I'm doing anything right. I have no natural knowledge of how to take care of Sienna.

Our dog, Shady, greets us at the door as we enter the house through the garage. His usual dance of excitement turns sour as I yell at him to go away. Shady is well trained, sleeps at the foot of our bed, and is the most lovable dog I know, yet he has turned into a wild animal who might harm Sienna. I bark at Kyle to put Shady out, fearful he might do something unpredictable. Kyle follows suit but looks at me hesitantly. He sets Sienna, still strapped into her car seat, on top of the dining room table. An image of her falling off the table shoots across my mind, and the thought brings me to tears.

Kyle hugs and consoles me. I don't have any words. These emotions and thoughts are foreign, like they aren't coming from me. I don't know who I am.

A week later, Sienna wakes up in the middle of night for a feeding. My nipples are scabbed over from a week and a half of breastfeeding day and night. The bedside clock reads 3:38. Nights are long and tough. Sleeping is no longer enjoyable because we're interrupted with screams and cries. I can't move. The thought of putting Sienna to my breast again is like ripping off a Band-Aid for twenty minutes straight. Kyle snores beside me. Her cries get louder, and I still can't move.

Kyle stirs, and he grabs my leg. "Em, the baby." Paralyzed, I don't move. Sienna's cries continue. Kyle sits up. "Em, the baby is crying; you need to feed her."

Crying softly, I tell Kyle, "I can't. I can't feed her."

"What? What do you mean?"

"My nipples, Kyle, look at them." I open my nursing nightgown to pull out a breast. The nursing bra is glued to my nipple in a wet circle. I cringe as I pull off the fabric and a creamy, pinkish goo oozes out. Kyle looks at it with disgust.

"It hurts so much."

"We got some formula from the hospital. We can give her that," Kyle suggests.

"No, breast milk is the best thing for Sienna. My mother did it, and that's what all the research says. I must do it, but...I can't move."

"We have to feed her, Em. I'll get the formula."

"No! Can you bring her to me? I'll do it; I can do it."

Kyle pauses, then gets up and brings Sienna to me. Tears roll down my face as I position her on my most engorged breast. Her mouth opens, and she latches on with a clamp. I wince. Kyle sees it. "Are you okay?"

"Yes." After ten minutes, I switch her to the other side. Same pain and tears. After she's drunk her fill, I feel better. There's an hour and a half of relief until the next feeding.

Two weeks after Sienna's birth, Kyle has a work trip. "I hate that I have to go, but my grandfather is giving me a hard time about making an impression of leadership in the company."

"I understand. I get it."

"You're doing better with the breast-feeding. I think you'll be fine. My mom is stopping by on Wednesday to check on you. I'll be back on Thursday evening."

"Yes, I'll be fine. Don't worry about us."

Kyle left on a Sunday morning, and I cried until the sun rose on Monday.

Back to my painting. I've made some headway with what I think will be a great piece. The hours roll by as the boats zoom past. There's nothing more empowering than creativity paired with productivity. The feeling is exhilarating.

I'm at a good stopping point and ready to experience something new. I waltz into the cabin and almost skip to the bedroom.

Okay, I do skip to the bedroom. I look through my clothes that I've arranged in the dresser drawers. I pick my favorite outfit, a long, flowy skirt with embroidery on it that I found at a thrift store. It was a gem of a find. Timing and location are the perfect combination for successful thrift store shopping. The shirt is simple and plain—an off-the-shoulder style that I wear with a sports bra. I put on my imitation Vans, and I'm out the door.

I'm struck by how much routine and the sameness of every day impacted my perception at home. Here I am, about to go up the steepest driveway I've ever encountered. My every day back home is the same, and my choices lead to the same results. This one is new. It appears to be a simple decision, but I've been sitting here for five minutes contemplating my next move.

The driveway is off the main road that circles the lake. Cars fly around the curve too fast to see them coming. Finally, I floor it to make it to the top, then, at the very top, slam on the brakes to keep from entering the main road. Little things can make life so much easier. A cul-de-sac is underrated.

My courage has surfaced, and my next move is set. Just as I'm about to floor the gas pedal, a loud truck rounds the curve and passes by. My heart goes to my throat and stays there.

Calm down; you're fine. To never drive out of this driveway is not an option. I must do it now. I step on the pedal, and the car revs and moves upward; the incline pulls me back in my seat as if I'm in a recliner. Just as I'm about to enter the road, I slam on the brakes. My body bounces forward. I'm right by the edge, and a car could come at any moment. I sit there and then floor it again, making a right turn onto the street, wheels squealing, flinging the car around. I straighten it out. I made it. It's over. A new moment. Let's get on with it.

The road is winding, and the bird wings in my stomach are flapping. I see the lake to my right out of the corner of my eye. Even from such a limited view, it's a sight that slices into my mind as pleasurable and relaxes the flapping. I slow my pace as I round the curves. Who cares if it makes the drive longer?

I approach an area that is townish. It's the end of the lake, and there's a beach, restaurants, and a marina. A familiar-looking building, perhaps a hotel, sits to the left. I pass by the beach and round a corner to see the welcome center on the right, just past the marina. I park there and head inside.

I grab for the doorknob just as the door swings open, barely missing my nose. No one is behind the swing, so I'm surprised and confused until I look down and see a child of about three years old storm out. Her mother is behind her yelling, "Stop, May! You'd better apologize to that lady."

May, paying no mind to her mother, keeps going into the parking lot. The mother huffs as she passes by me. "Oooh... I'm sorry. She's driving me crazy." I hear the mother continue behind me. "May, no dessert for you today. No, ma'am."

I walk forward and see an elderly lady sitting at a counter, surrounded by brochures. She says nothing, just stares as I walk toward her. When I reach her, I say, "Hi, I just wanted to get some information about the area. This is the first time I've been here."

She looks at me for an awkward moment, as if she didn't hear me, and then replies, "Sure. These brochures will tell you all about the area."

"Oh, okay. Can you tell me a little bit about Lake Lure and maybe recommend some places to visit?"

As I'm asking the question, her eyes dart down as though she's staring at something else that has caught her attention. She looks back up. "Well, what do you like to do?"

"The marina next door, do they rent boats? Or are they privately owned?"

"Oh, you can rent them. Here's the brochure." She grabs a brochure and shoves it out for me to take.

"Thanks."

I catch a glimpse of some hiking brochures and catch her looking down again. "What's the most popular hiking trail around here?"

Once again, a long pause, and then, "I would say Chimney Rock State Park on Rumbling Bald Mountain, right up the street, but that's just what I hear. I can't speak for everyone." She stacks three brochures and hands them to me.

"I passed by an Italian restaurant before getting to the beach. Do you like it? Would you recommend it?"

A pause and then, with no enthusiasm, she says, "Oh, yes. It's good." Once again, she looks down at something and then back up. I expect her to hand me another stack of brochures, but she just stares at me, anticipating another question.

"Well...thank you for the brochures. Have a nice day."

For the first time, she smiles big, apparently eager to see me leave. "You too, hon. Enjoy your time here."

I turn with the stack of brochures in my hand and walk toward the exit. When I grab the door to open it, I look back. The lady picks up a book, turns a page, and starts reading. I smile to myself and continue out to my car. Instead of getting in, I head toward the marina.

The area looks like it's been a tourist location for a while, with some great local involvement and perks. Kind of dated, yet preserved. The sun is shining. The day is vibrant and alive. The lake from this side twinkles while the mountains lie beside it, resting with contrasting depth.

I walk toward where I see people lining up on the dock. A small convenience store borders it, and when I walk in, two middle-aged women are working the cash registers and chatting with customers. I look around the store. A few customers are checking out, a child is studying the candy aisle, and there's a police officer with his back turned toward me leaning against the bait fridge eating a Nutter Butter ice cream and watching the people lining up on the dock. I smile to myself. *Not a donut, but an ice cream splurge. What a way to challenge the cliché.*

I wait for the customers to check out and walk up to the cashier. "Hi. I'd like to find out about your boat rentals."

The woman replies, "Whatcha looking for? Private boats or our guided tour of the lake?"

I think for a moment and then respond, "How about the guided tour?"

"That's fifteen dollars per adult, about a one-hour trip..."

I look to my right, and I'm caught off guard because the police officer is looking right at me. He must have walked to the freezer while I was talking, and he's now leaning up against it, looking at me while he finishes his ice cream. His demeanor is arrogant. I look back at the woman, who notices my distraction. She pauses and continues. "You have to make reservations typically a day ahead of time. We are all booked for today."

"Can I make reservations online or over the phone?"

"You can call us."

I don't like the way the police officer is looking at me. I feel like I'm being accused of something. An overpowering wave of guilt washes over me.

I thank the woman and make my way out of the store. I look back to see what he's doing, and he walks to the entry and leans against the doorframe, watching me. *Shit, why is he watching me?* I fast walk toward my car and get in. I see signs pointing toward Chimney Rock. It's not far from here. The wings are back with a vengeance. I want to vomit.

And then it dawns on me; that was the police officer who stopped me while I was driving to the rental on Friday. My heart calms. *Silly me.* He recognizes me, but maybe he can't place me. Or maybe he does remember me. I'm relieved, but something is still off.

CHAPTER 15:

I look over the patio of Burntshirt, a local winery. On such a gorgeous day, with a great view of Chimney Rock, a flock of people wait by the door. One two-top table is available, half inside, half outside. "Perfect," I tell the hostess.

I scurried through town not like your typical tourist would, meandering through the shops stuffed full of Chimney Rock merchandise. Instead, I walked quickly past the knickknacks, T-shirts, and homemade jellies. There were mobs of people walking in and out of stores and restaurants. I was pleased to come across the label of the wine I drank last night plastered on a sign in front of the restaurant.

The waitress is likely in her fifties, with a weathered, yet calming, smoker's voice. Something about the raspy tone of smokers makes me assume that they're down-to-earth people. An attractive lady, cheeks pink with sunburn, she introduces herself as Darby. "What can I get ya to drink, hon?"

Nervous and chatty, I'm craving the comfort of familiarity in someone else. I ask her right away, "How are you today? You been busy?"

She looks at her pad of paper, smiles, and looks up at me. "It's been nonstop on the weekends since spring break. Just jam-packed, but it's better that way. The time flies by."

I flash a smile and look at the menu. "I would love to do a wine tasting and get some of the small plates. For food, what do you recommend?"

Darby relaxes her arms to her sides and looks up as if this will help jog her brain better. "Well, I love the mac and cheese and the brussels sprouts, and the trout is really popular."

"I'm starving, so I'll take all of that, and add some grits."

"Okay. What wines do you want to taste?" I hand her my slip of paper with all the wines that I chose.

"Can you bring me some water too?"

"Sure thing, hon. I'll be right back with your water."

Darby leaves and returns soon after with a glass of water. "You here on vacation?" She asks as she sets the sweaty glass down.

"Yep. I've rented a place for a month on the lake. I'm getting some painting done for an upcoming exhibit."

Why did I just tell her all that? I'm usually not very forthcoming about my career. Surprisingly for me, I said it with conviction and pride in myself. It's one of those professions where you need to be famous to have others recognize it as a legit career. In the same breath, you also get praised for having the balls to do it as a full-time career choice.

"You're an artist? Cool! What kind of art do you do?"

"I mainly paint and draw."

Darby smiles. "There's a gallery up the way, headed toward Asheville, if you want to check out some of the local artists around here. There are some good ones."

"Okay, I might check it out."

"Let me grab your wine. I see they have it ready for you at the bar."

I turn toward the massive mountain that has lent itself as a backdrop to the quaint town of Chimney Rock. The distant rushing of water from the Broad River acts as an undertone of relaxing white noise. The day couldn't get any better. That realization brings chills to my arms as a slight breeze tickles my skin.

Darby brings a flight of the five different wines that I chose, and the dishes that I ordered soon follow. I enjoy the ambience as

I eat and sip the wine. It doesn't take long until the buzz hits my head, and the wine-induced euphoria runs through my veins. It heightens my mood and stimulates my need to connect. Looking around the patio, I notice at the table next to me a Lab mix lying down and looking up at its owner while wagging its tail. The family of four talks among themselves.

Darby walks up and interrupts my musing. "Where ya staying on the lake? I know most places; my brother has a place on the water." At that moment, I'm reminded of what the police officer said on Friday when I drove in. *What was it? The Howard place?*

I'm hesitant to mention it, given the police officer's reaction. "Well, I rented it from the Lake Lure Rental Company. Maybe you knew the previous owner. The Howard place?"

A blank look takes over her face, and her tone and energy shift. She sends me a nervous smile. "Looks like you need some more water. I'll get you some." She goes to the water station, whispers something to another waitress, then turns to look at me and turns back. *What's going on?*

Darby returns with a water pitcher and a fresh smile on her face, recharged and playing the part. As she refills my glass, I ask, "Is there something that happened to the Howards' house? You seemed a little spooked when I mentioned it."

Her smile freezes. "I don't know the place."

Liar.

Her words come out edgy and different from the way she was speaking to me before. "There have been several renovations of cabins in the past two years. I'm sure it's one of them. This place has exploded recently. I liked it better when it was a hidden gem." She knows something and is refusing to tell me. But why?

Just as I'm about to ask another question, I see a familiar face walking toward my table. Darby notices my distraction and takes the opportunity to leave.

It's the neighbor, Tom, and he's walking beside a striking woman around his age. He looks at me and whispers to the woman, then waves while he walks up.

"Well, hello there. Emily, right?"

"Yes, um, Tom, nice to see you again."

"Well, I see that you're fitting right in and making yourself at home here."

"It was the bottle of wine you gave me. I had to come and taste more. Thank you again for the wine and gifts."

Tom turns and introduces his wife, Carol. I'm struck by her beauty. She's in her late sixties I guess, and her age looks like it should on her. Her silver hair and porcelain white skin glow. She's wearing loose slacks with a shirt and cardigan, all flattering to her figure. Her jewelry pops, and her blue eyes stand out. A slow smile crosses her face.

"Nice to meet you, Carol. Tom speaks highly of you."

"Oh, he knows better. By now, he knows any petty complaints will come back to me before the sun goes down. Tom told me you're renting next door to us. The house was recently sold. We had no idea it was going to be a rental."

"Yes, thank you for the gifts. I'll leave the towel there. Tom told me to enjoy them. I hope that's okay with you."

"Of course. Gifts are meant to be enjoyed, and it's an excuse to meet people. Tom didn't tell me that you're a looker. Tom, why are you keeping secrets from me?"

"Well, thanks. Tom didn't tell me that you're a looker either."

Tom laughs. "See, I knew you two would like each other. She's an artist, too, Carol."

"Yes, I heard. Let's meet for coffee tomorrow, talk art, and I'll tell you some stories." She winks at me.

Something about Carol's beauty and directness have taken me by surprise. I have a strong desire to know this lady. Plus, they must know about the history of the rental. If I get close to Carol,

I'll be able to find out why I'm getting such odd vibes about the previous owners of the house. With genuine excitement, I respond, "Absolutely."

"Great. I'll bring my famous coffee cake to share. How does nine a.m. sound?"

"That's perfect."

"Well, we're here to meet our friends. They have a table inside. It was nice meeting you, Emily. I'll see you tomorrow morning. Enjoy the rest of your day."

They walk off.

I'm elated at the interaction. A sense of depth and mystery with a splash of comfort is starting to take root. The inspiration is bubbling out of me. There's nothing like a saucy story that doesn't involve me that distracts me from myself and ignites inspiration. I pay the check.

Darby is more distant than before, but she comments about Carol and Tom when she hands me the bill, tells me how nice they are, the most sociable couple in town, and how Tom adores Carol.

Once I get to the house, I walk out to the porch and gratefully breathe in the peace this place is giving me. I pour the last glass of wine from the bottle they gave me and sit and look out onto the lake. The blank canvas calls my name, and I move to my easel and start to paint. My strokes follow a rhythm. It's effortless, and my heart sings. When the pace lessens and the creative juices dry up, I look at my watch and see it's midnight. I drink a glass of water and fall into bed, my sleep peaceful.

CHAPTER 16:

I wake up expecting a hangover, but to my surprise, I feel refreshed. The good day before grants me a pass for today. Perhaps the flooding of endorphins yesterday compared to the usual lack of them I usually experience buffered the hangover. I look at the clock: 7:33. It's perfect timing. Time to get ready for the day. I put on a comfy dress, brush my teeth, and dab on a little makeup.

I prepare a cup of coffee, take it to the porch, and examine the work I did the night before. I'm struck by the painting. Every artist has a stroke style and a signature way of painting once they settle into it; however, I've never seen this painting style come out of me before. It's peculiar. While the coffee helps my brain wake up, I stare at the painting. The strokes from last night look choreographed, like my hand went along for the ride. Where did this come from? I decide not to put too much thought into it. As soon as I finish my usual dose of caffeine, I'm off and painting. The same phenomenon happens again. It's like learning how to ride a bike and coasting down a hill at full speed.

I'm interrupted by a knock at the door. I'm elated by my productivity and the fluidity of my work as I put the brush down. The happiness running through me feels so odd. I'm in a body I haven't been in for a long time.

When I swing open the door, I find Carol looking more beautiful than I remembered.

"Hi, there. Please come in." I can feel the smile on my face, and the invitation is so welcoming that I don't know who I am anymore, but it feels confident, and I like it. I want to keep this new person going.

Carol grabs me in a hug. "Glad we could meet up." She enters the cabin and looks around. "It was renovated before the previous owner took over, and I've peeked inside before, but I haven't seen the final results. Can I look around?"

I show Carol around, and we pass by the stairs going down to the basement. I laugh. "I haven't ventured down there yet, but from the outside it appears to be original and not finished. I need to do some laundry, but I'm not looking forward to venturing into a creepy basement."

She seems impressed by the house. "I like what they did. They kept it simple and prioritized what's important: the lake view."

She looks out onto the lake and sighs. "It's amazing. I live just next door, and this perspective of the lake is completely different from ours. I have to say this view is more intriguing."

"That's what got me here to begin with. The view entertains me for hours on end."

We're back in the kitchen, where she left the coffee cake on the counter. "Do you have a knife I can cut this with?"

"Yes, of course. Can I make you some coffee?"

"Sure, I drink it black."

I hand her a knife, and she puts slices of the coffee cake onto plates. With our cups of coffee and plates in hand, we move out to the porch and settle back into the chairs looking out onto the lake. I don't have my typical social anxiety from being with someone I don't know. I thought I'd feel the judgmental vibe I usually get from women, looking me up and down, judging what I'm wearing, asking what my story is, why this, why that, parenting complaints, and so on, but Carol seems less judgmental and more interesting to me. She's not really interrogating me; I want to know more about her.

"So where are you originally from?" I ask her.

"Tom and I are from Asheville. I was a high school art teacher, and Tom traveled a lot selling pharmaceuticals. We've been retired for years now. We bought our place a few years before we retired. I love it here. We have great friends, and life is good. Asheville isn't too far away, and it's peaceful. So...what about you? Where are you from?"

"Atlanta. This is the first time I've been here, but I see why you love it so much. So...did you own the house when the Howards lived here?" I couldn't wait to ask the question.

"Oh, you've already heard about the Howards. Interesting. They moved out a year before we bought our house, and it stayed vacant forever. About five years ago, an investor renovated it and sold it to the current owner. You don't believe all the crazy things they say about this house, do you? It's absurd. I don't believe it for a minute."

"That's exactly why I asked. No one has told me anything. I was hoping you'd fill me in."

"Just your average gossip. The family was odd. They suddenly left town, and no one knew where they went. That's how gossip begins. People fill in the gaps with their own stories, and by the time it's circled around town, they're devil worshippers, they're possessed by demons, the house is haunted, they're witches, Mr. Howard was abusive, Mrs. Howard was mentally ill, they were not to be trusted, or they were all taking drugs. The weirdest part is, not one person knows where they went. They disappeared, for sure. I've lost count of the different stories, and now I tell people to shut up about it when I'm around. It's all hearsay. 'Don't fill my head full of crap,' I tell them." She laughs.

"Why did the house sit vacant for so long?"

"Because of that very reason—the stories. Someone saw them drive off at nine a.m. on a Saturday morning, and they never came back. That's the only fact that's confirmed. If I'd been here and known them, I would have tracked them down. I would never have let them disappear like that. And I wouldn't have created stories. I'm not saying nobody had reason to question, but I haven't heard one account with actual evidence. All just crap gossip. When people come to me with their ridiculous stories about the family, I say, 'Why did you let them go without knowing who they are? So you can make up stories about them?' They shut up when I say that."

I like Carol. She calls out the BS, and she's not afraid to speak her mind and put people in their place. "How do people respond when you say that?"

"They know me and know better. I volunteer for everything and host so many gatherings. I've earned their respect. Plus, I don't give a damn what people think about me. I say what I want. People tend to like you more when you create boundaries, trust me. They might get offended for a week, but they still come to my full moon parties and invite me to their gatherings."

"Should I be scared or freaked out about the cabin?"

"I would never have said anything if you hadn't asked. Do you feel like there's something dangerous about this place?"

I think about the question and realize I actually feel comfortable here. "No. I feel safe, productive, and happier than usual. Well, except for the freaky basement. But every old house needs to have a creepy part to it, right? For nostalgia."

"Okay, then don't worry about the Howards. Put it out of your mind and think about your art."

I'm convinced she's right.

She gestures toward the lake. "How about another cup of coffee and we take it out on the dock? Let's talk art. I'll tell you some true stories about the people around here. Like my neighbors, Rick and Gary, who can't stop getting drunk and accidentally ending up in bed with each other's wives."

I choke on my coffee cake. "What? What do you mean accidentally?"

"Right, it's an accident." She winks at me.

I'm intrigued. It's trash conversation about people I don't know, but I want to hear it. I prepare us each another cup of coffee, and we walk down to the dock and sit in the two Adirondack chairs facing the cove.

"Not to stir something up, but I thought you didn't like to gossip about people?"

She laughs. "I never said I didn't want to talk about people when I have something real to talk about. Are you serious? I just don't like making up stories about people when there's no proof. The Howards could have been introverts for all I know. I would have gotten to the bottom of it, that's all. Like catching Rick and Gary switching homes at six in the morning."

I'm shocked and so invested. "What the hell? How do you know for sure?"

"First of all, you can hear everything echoing off the water at that hour."

She points to the house on the right next to her house. "That's Gary and Leslie's house. They have four kids." Then she points to the house next to my cabin on the left. "That's Rick and Cynthia's house. They have two girls." She takes a sip from her mug. "I was sitting on my dock drinking coffee when I heard Rick and Gary in their boats, laughing and talking, still drunk likely, as they passed each other on their way home. Rick yelled out, 'How was fucking my wife last night?' Gary said, 'We did it in the hot tub, man. You're going to want to drain that.' They were laughing at each other, and Rick asked Gary if Cynthia gave him a blow job. Then, to their dismay, they looked over and saw me staring at them with a grin on my face. I could tell Rick was mortified. He waved and said, 'Hey, Carol, you're up early.' That stopped their laughter pretty quickly. You know, I was in heaven seeing it play out. I always suspected funny business with those families." She makes a sarcastic face. "But I didn't want them to feel bad about their scandalous behavior. So I said, 'I see you both accidentally slept over at the wrong house. It happens to the best of us.' Gary said, 'We were just kidding around; we drank too much last night.' They gave nervous laughs and mouthed *oh fuck* to each other. Like I didn't see that either."

I'm dying laughing at this point. My stomach hurts. Carol is laughing too. There's something about hearing this story that makes me feel normal and closer to Carol. She has a knack for being with people.

I ask, "Did anything else happen? What about the wives?"

"Umm, maybe something was said to them, because I've invited them to many events, but they always have something going on—both families. They used to hang out with everyone. They'll wave at me from their docks now, but that's it." She pauses for a moment. "Come to think of it, Leslie doesn't seem to give a damn. She came to my last full moon party. Actually, I kind of like her more for not hiding. It makes her more real, and personally, I don't give a shit what they do." She starts laughing.

"Did you tell anyone?"

"I told Tom, of course, and he told me about some coworker and his wife a while back who were into that sort of thing, but no, no one else. I felt you were safe. It'll be a fun secret to know if you meet them. You seem like you'll take it the right way."

Carol sips her coffee. "So, are you married? Do you have kids?"

Normally the questions would be a sore spot, but Carol's attitude toward people seems accepting, so I tell her the truth, at least part of it. "I've been divorced for over thirteen years; we had a daughter together."

Carol seems cautious. "Oh, I see. Did you remarry ever? Do you have a partner?"

"No, I'm not into having a relationship, really. Kind of done with that."

She doesn't ask me more about Sienna, and I think that's weird. "Well, I guess that's a thing these days. If Tom dies tomorrow, I'm moving on as quickly as possible. I don't like being alone. Tom knows it too. He jokes that I would go for a younger man, and I just might." She laughs.

"So...you taught art in high school, and Tom said you still do art. What do you like to do?"

"I like to paint and sketch. I'm also into interior decorating for close friends who are decorating-challenged. That's fun. If you want to see some of my stuff, why don't you come over for dinner tomorrow night?"

I was surprised by the invitation, but I liked Carol. "Sure, I'd love to have dinner with you and Tom."

I feel like a normal human being, a person who wants to be a part of something else, be with people. I feel healthy.

I'm pulled from my thoughts by Carol's next words.

"Oh, I see what you mean by a creepy basement." She's looking back toward the house. We head over and look through the basement windows. The inside seems dark, unfinished, and cobwebs span every windowsill. It's cluttered with life jackets, oars, old kayaks, and rafts.

We head back up to the porch, and she stops to look at my canvas. She just stares at it for a few long seconds, then says, "Wow, I can't wait to see this painting finished." She gives me a smile and walks over to set her coffee cup in the kitchen sink. "I need to get going. I'm teaching my friend how to watercolor while she's recovering from surgery. We eat at six like clockwork. You should come at five. I see you like wine. Are you allergic to anything?"

"Nope."

"Good, because I don't want to send you to the hospital. See you tomorrow at five."

Carol leaves, and I miss her already. I needed the interaction.

I eat more coffee cake, then start painting again. Hours fly by, and I burn time. I feel like I'm not on planet Earth. There is an energetic bubble surrounding me in this place. I like it. Interactions flow, and I fit in here.

I was pregnant and in love. I was scared shitless, but I was happy and naive. Sienna growing inside me felt spectacular, like I could do something novel and beautiful. Daydreaming consisted of picturing how smart and pretty she would be. I did everything right, according to every book I read. I listened to the doctors and ate the right things. I was young and energetic. I glowed like pregnant women glow. Kyle and I still made love all the time. The relationship had reached a new level. We got closer.

We replaced late-night parties, smoking, and screwing whenever we were somewhat alone with watching interesting movies and delving into foreign films. It was a great way to pass the time, time that seemed to tick along more slowly than usual. Life trying to tell me to get my shit together because it was about to shatter everything I thought I knew about myself.

We went to see a movie, one Kyle was on the fence about. I fell in love with it from the opening scene.

When we got back to the car, I asked Kyle, "Did you like it?"

"Yeah, it was good. Better than I thought it would be. I loved it from the beginning."

I went on about it for a while until I realized Kyle was looking at me, smiling.

"What?"

"Nothing. I just haven't seen you so excited about a movie before."

"I don't know; it revived me." And it had.

Kyle leaned over, and we kissed. By this point in our relationship, we had kissed a million times. But there was something special about this kiss. My insides were touched, and something else had been pulled out of me. It was as if we had never kissed before, and I wasn't the same person. Those moments are rare, and they don't last.

I come back to the present, but the memory leaves me with a sour feeling in my gut. The juxtaposition of happiness before children and how I could understand life then to how drastically it changed after giving birth. It's cruel, really.

CHAPTER 17:

I managed to stay wine dry for a day, which is great. I'm lying in bed feeling fulfilled, checking my texts, when I hear a noise coming from outside my bedroom.

At first, my mind wants to discount the sound. I didn't really hear anything. But there it is again. It's a scratching noise, and it's repetitive. It doesn't sound like wind moving things around, but something a living thing would make. I sit there frozen in bed. I'm scared to see what's on the other side of the door. There it is again, and again. I have to do something; otherwise, I won't sleep.

First step is to open the bedroom door. It's the only way I'll be able to get a better gauge of the sound. Should I text someone before I do it? Just in case something happens to me?

I'll text Chastain. Arin isn't great at returning texts or looking at her phone. Chastain stays attached. I start to text her and realize anything I say would cause distress, since she's so far away. I don't want to freak her out. I try:

Hey Chas, I hear a noise and I'm going to check it out, just putting you on alert. It's probably nothing.

I can't freaking send that. I delete it, then try:
Hi Chas, I'm a little scared. Can you call me while I go and walk through my cabin. No reason, just me being scared.

I debate with myself for a long minute before I finally hit send. Meanwhile, I keep hearing the noise.

I wait for what seems like an eternity but is only five minutes before I call her. She doesn't answer. *You have got to be kidding me.*

I can't remember a time that she didn't answer, but I'm mainly a texter. She's the caller. I'm beside myself frightened. She's not answering, and I can't sit here all night wondering. I finally grab the umbrella I'd left leaning against the wall—it's a weapon of sorts, right?—walk over, grab the knob, and swing the door open. I jump when I see the black coatrack in the corner. It's been there the whole time, nothing different, but my nervous system is cranked up to high alert. It's a tiny relief to see nothing out of the ordinary.

I leave the door open and run back to bed, trying to calm myself as I listen. I hear it again, and this time I'm able to get a direction. It's coming from the kitchen. Shit. Shit. I take a deep breath and realize I have to go out there and see what it is.

My brain starts thinking of the worst-case scenario. The sound gets louder, and I can't take it anymore. I venture out with the umbrella in tow, the light from the bedroom barely enough to see by. I turn right and then head straight down the hallway. I see my reflection in the glass doors out to the porch, and my heart jumps again...ugh. Annoyed by my immature jumpiness, I move forward. I hear the sound again and round the corner past the steps leading to the basement. A quick peek down there to rule it out, and sure enough, there's nothing on the steps or at the bottom of them. The door is closed, as usual. Another triumph. I get past the stairs and have a full view of the kitchen, only to find nothing there. I blink. I look over to the living room, to the back porch, again to the kitchen. I swear I heard it from this direction.

At this point, I need to figure this out, so I run back to the guest bedroom that faces my bedroom and turn on the light... nothing. I get to the bathroom, light on, not a damn thing. I hear the sound again, and now I think it might be coming from the basement.

Fear creeps through my veins and across my skin, goosebumps pop up, and the hair on my head seems to increase in volume. I turn again and head toward the stairs, moving in slow motion. I hear the noise, and I stop at the top of the stairs leading down to the basement. I don't see anything, but it seems the noise is now coming from behind the basement door.

I have to make a decision. My chest is bouncing to the rhythm of my quickened heartbeat. I must go down those stairs. I gulp and start my descent, and something catches my eye. Was that a creature darting away? I whip my head around to look back at the kitchen, head back up the stairs. I know I saw something in the kitchen, but now it's gone.

I'm sweating with nervousness, and the sudden quiet isn't helping. All of a sudden, something pops up between the stovetop and the back of the oven, a tiny space just big enough for a mouse to fit through and grab any food left lying out. The little guy dashes off the stovetop toward a bag of popcorn, to the hole ripped in the bag, popcorn spilling out. He grabs a couple of pieces, stuffs them in his mouth, and scuttles back to the stovetop. He's almost back in hiding when my phone blasts out a ring. I let out a short scream, and the mouse freezes, turns to look at me, then takes off for its secret escape route.

It's Chastain, of course. The timing is unreal. Out of breath, I answer, "Hi, Chas! How are you?"

She pauses for a second. "Em? Are you all right? You sound like you're running."

I can feel the adrenaline leaving my body at the sound of her voice. "I'm fine. You're not going to believe this."

"WHAT? I was putting the girls down. I called you as soon as I read your text."

"I didn't text you the full truth. I kept hearing this noise in the kitchen, and before I went to see what was causing the noise, I texted you just in case something happened."

"Oh my God. See, I told you! Please tell me you were just imagining things."

"No, it's not what you think. It was a freaking mouse. You have no idea how scared I was. I'm so relieved, and you called right when I saw the little monster. Can you believe it?"

Chastain laughs. "I knew it. It's freaky being alone in a cabin in a place you don't know. If it was me, I'd be calling you every night before I went to bed, wondering if there was someone in the kitchen. So how is the cabin?"

"It's great. I'm painting again, sketching every day. I've met the next-door neighbors, Tom and Carol. They're great. I'm having dinner with them tomorrow. The cabin, the view, everything is better than I thought. It's just..."

"It's just what?"

"Well, the washer and dryer are in the basement. It's creepy as fuck, even the steps going down to it. I still haven't gone down there, but in the next couple of days, I need to do laundry."

"See, I knew there was a catch. I say you don't do your laundry. Don't do it. Wear your clothes over and over. Ain't nobody gonna care. I would be washin' my clothes in the sink and hangin' them up like Granny used to do."

I laugh. "You know that might not be a bad plan."

I say this for conversation purposes. I'll go down there eventually. The basement, as scary as it seems, is calling me. I have to find out that everything is only in my head so I can rest better at night. The stairs want me to go down them. I can feel it.

"Okay, well, do you need me to talk to you for a while longer? Are you still freaked out?"

"No, I'm good. It's funny now. I'll rest easy tonight."

"Good. I'm happy you're having a good time. Have you talked to Arin since you've been there?

"No. I texted her when I got here, but that's all. She's busy, busy. Thanks, Chas. I'll talk to you later."

"Remember, don't go down into that basement. I can't leave my kids, so you're on your own if you go down there. I can't handle sitting here on the phone and listening to you creep down those stairs to face your death."

Laughing, I respond, "Okay, Chas, you got it."

I hang up, clean up the popcorn and head to bed. I sleep hard.

CHAPTER 18:

My belly wakes me up in the morning and pulls me out of bed, but my legs carry me to my unfinished canvas. My arm rises. I put paint on a brush. What's happening here? I set the brush down and pull myself away from the stool. I need coffee. That's the first thing I do every day, but today my body doesn't want to listen.

I push myself to move toward the kitchen, but something pulls me back toward the stool. I fight it. Coffee first. It's as if I'm going in slow motion. My brain is lagging, and my body feels weighted down. I make a cup of coffee, but before I can take a sip, the force pulls me back to the stool, coffee forgotten on the counter. I trip and land on the floor with a thud. My body stands up, walks over, and sits down on the stool. My arm paints and paints with broad quick strokes. The hours fly by, the clock speeds up. My arm moves to the momentum of the clock. I paint for hours, several different paintings, before I stop. The paintbrush drops from my aching hand, which seems to have been numb all along, and I can just now feel it. The force pulling me in is satisfied. I'm exhausted and drag myself to the couch in the living room. My mind blanks for a while, and then I begin to think about the thing that has been an irritating buzz in the back of my head.

The stairs going to the basement. It's as if they aren't part of the house. They give insight into how old the house really is. They stop the flow of the house, and the view downward looks as if you're going down to a dungeon, to a place of death, where murder happens. An imagination field day that knows no end to its psychological torture.

Why didn't the owner at least update the stairs and the door at the bottom? The doorknob is old, and I don't know if it's locked. In daytime, the cabin is light, airy, and energetic, whereas nighttime conjures vulnerability.

After walking by the stairs several times, back and forth, I force myself to stop. I need to check if the door is locked. Sleeping will be problematic if I don't know for sure that the door is secured. I'm kicking myself for not doing it earlier in the day when the sun was high. Imagination is tamed by light; nothing horrific can happen when the sun is bright, so we're fooled.

Each step creaks as I put my weight on it. *Of course they do.* The pitch is steep, and each tread is narrow. I feel heavier than usual, and there is a give, like they could cave in at any time. Halfway down, I feel the change in temperature. It gets cooler with each step. The walls, once likely white, have a tarnished, aged look to them, with pencil scribbles from decades of kids writing on them. I get stuck on a scribble of a game of hangman. The word is "trouble."

The light from the kitchen is dim, shadowed by the narrow walls of the staircase. The smell is a dusty corner in an antique shop. I have an epiphany as I descend to the bottom. *This house represents who I am.* Renovated on the outside, quite attractive looking, yet the stairs within me take me to cryptic places, best entered with a friend beside me whose hand I can squeeze for comfort.

I reach the bottom, and looking back up, the stairs seem longer and steeper from the bottom than from the top. What if there's a man on the other side of this door? Running up the stairs would be tough. What if there's a hungry bear?

I reach for the doorknob, and when I touch it, it feels like ice. I turn it, and the door flies wide open. A cold breeze gusts past my face, blowing my hair back.

Beyond the door, it's completely dark, and all I can detect is a subtle, rancid, rotting smell. An insidious fear creeps up my spine to the base of my neck, where I feel my hair stand up. I pull the door and hear it latch. I turn to run up the stairs, but my momentum and the narrow treads cause me to lose my footing halfway up. I fall to my knees and slide down, one by one.

I get up, knees red, and trot back upstairs, lengthening my stride. When I arrive at the top, I turn to look back, feeling as if something is following me and about to catch up, but I see nothing, only the closed door and the stairs leading to it. Stagnant, nothing moving except my pounding heart and my rising and falling chest. I am alone.

CHAPTER 19:

I'm standing in front of one of my paintings. I come alert, as if snapping out of a trance. It feels like hours have passed, though I have no clue how long I've been here. My arm is sore. I glance at my watch. I only have an hour until Tom and Carol's dinner. I shake my head and head to the bathroom to get ready.

I decide to dress up in a black dress, adding red lipstick and a little more makeup than usual. I grab a bottle of wine, and I'm out the door. A minute later, I'm knocking.

When Tom opens the door, I catch a wave of warmth mixed with an aroma of hours spent cooking, quite the invitation. Tom greets me with a smile and says, "Oh, you again?" He chuckles to himself like he didn't care if I thought it was funny or not.

I join his laughter. "Hi, me again. I brought a bottle of wine. My favorite."

"That's perfect. We just opened a bottle. Carol is making her famous pot roast."

We walk into the kitchen together, and Carol is stirring something on the stovetop. She looks up, smiles big, and turns enough for me to see she's wearing an apron that reads *You'll eat what I serve you, Bitch*. I look at it and laugh.

"Oh, I got this at one of the stores in town. When I was full force in menopause, I stopped caring about everyone's diet, so you either ate what I cooked or starved at my house. A doctor's note was the only way you didn't get the evil eye from me. Speaking of, what is your diet? No, no, let me guess... Vegan or gluten-free?"

"Truthfully, I eat what's cheapest and healthiest. Pasta is a go-to meal, so not gluten-free, but not a lot of meat."

"Well, today is your lucky day. We're having pot roast, glazed carrots, roasted potatoes, green beans, and cornbread. I made a berry cobbler for dessert."

"That sounds so good. I can't remember the last time I had someone cook for me like this."

Carol hands me a glass of wine. For the first time in a long time, I don't feel the need to drink it down. Carol turns to Tom, "Watch the green beans on the stovetop, will ya? Give 'em a couple whirl-arounds." Tom nods in agreement.

Carol guides me around the house. It's larger than mine and two stories. Their decor is less of a minimalist look, more eclectic, but it's pleasing to the eye. Nooks and crannies reveal souvenirs from trips that Tom and Carol have taken, and there are lots of off-the-beaten-path antiques with colors and patterns I can't quite grasp. One corner is dedicated to black-and-white photos and framed insects. "I see you like insects."

Carol snickers. "Aren't they fascinating, the way their bodies form shapes, especially flattened? They're geometric and linear."

I see a white butterfly with a wingspan that looks larger than a foot. I know it must be real, but its size is shocking.

"Is this a real butterfly?"

Carol smiles. "It's real, but it's not a butterfly. It's called a white witch moth. Found it framed like this when we went to Texas. I had to have it. Isn't she gorgeous?"

I nod and stare at it, thinking back to my boxed black butterfly, and a shiver runs down my spine. I move on to photos of her son, her granddaughter, and generations of family members. She takes me to her art studio toward the back of the house. There are floor-to-ceiling windows on the side facing the lake. The room has lots of natural light, and the paintings are stacked against each other. I see a lot of landscapes of lakes, fields, trees, and forests with tall trees...lots and lots of trees. Her fascination with trees is notable. There are only a few paintings of people, so they stand out.

"What's your fascination with trees and forests?"

"It's obvious, isn't it? I spent a lot of time in the woods when I was growing up. Playing, building forts, following my older brother. I also got lost one time, and they had to send out a search party to come find me. I went too far from the trail, and I lost track of time. I imagined all sorts of things, like I was Gretel, and I would come across a house made of candy. I thought I could live on my own and find another lost boy, and we would create a family in the woods. Before I knew it, I was lost. It was the most exhilarating and scary thing I experienced as a child. When I realized I couldn't find my way back, it was already getting dark. It was pitch black when they found me around eleven, five hours past dinnertime, which was when I was due back."

"Did anything dangerous happen while you were out there?"

"There could have been bears, snakes, and tons of other creatures ready to have me, but no. I had no fears as a child—nothing came after me. At first, I felt a little rebellious, like no one knew where I was—free from my family, a feral child. Then it got real. No one was coming. It was my brother who found me. He had gone that far into the woods before, and... Well, we were siblings, so he knew me. He was madder at me than anyone else was. Our parents said I could only go into the woods if my brother was with me from then on. He didn't let me go with him for over a year, but that didn't really stop me. I secretly followed him all the time."

Carol thumbs through several paintings to one with a tiny child sitting on a tree branch among oversized trees.

"You climbed a tree?"

"Yes. My brother told me if I ever got lost to climb a tree. It was safer there. I had leverage to see better, yell out for help, and hide from potential predators. He really didn't want me getting lost, though. I don't think he ever forgave me."

Carol grabs a sketchbook and brings it over to me. Interested, I open it and thumb through the pages.

Just as I'm about to ask a question, we hear Tom call out, "Carol, timer just went off."

"Oh, good lord, it's time."

I smile and follow Carol into the dining room, where plates and napkins are set out. Everything is on the table, serving utensils at the ready. Carol and Tom are obviously expert dinner entertainers. I glance at my watch, and my butt hits the chair at six on the dot. *Damn, they're good.*

"I'm impressed with your timeliness; it's exactly six."

Tom responds, "Years and years of practice and doing it wrong, and we agreed that we like to do things on time."

Carol puts her hand on his shoulder. "Well, it was more of a struggle for me, since I'm the main cook, but I came around. It was important to Tom, and so the deal was when I scream for him, he must come to my rescue. Only now we don't have to do that anymore. He senses when I'm going to lose it before it happens these days."

They laugh together, and Carol says, "I trained him, so we're almost equal, but really I enjoy cooking, so I want to do most of it."

He covers her hand with his. "I'm just appreciative that my wife is the prettiest, best cook on Lake Lure. I'm the luckiest man alive."

Their display of love seems genuine. I can't remember a time when I've seen an older couple so much in love, or at least show respect and appreciation for one another. It's usually the year-into-the-relationship, just-married, before-kids couples that show affection like this. Couples at their age are more likely to avoid each other and nag at one another. Sort of like, *Why would we separate at this age, with all this time under our belts*?

The long-term relationships I've seen are more sarcastic, not loving. Not at that age and years in. It's logical to stay with a partner while growing older, for obvious reasons like taking care of each other and having companionship, but to still show genuine love... I'm not completely convinced they're being honest—not really. I flash a smile that I hope says *that's sweet* to them.

Dinner conversation continues. Tom pours us both wine while we talk about some of the things happening in town. They share with me their schedule full of activities that keep them occupied. Tom plays golf twice a week with other retirees. Both love talking about being retired and how it's so important to keep yourself busy with projects, trips, parties, reading, and boating, and how being somewhere fun for grandkids is key to having your children visit more often.

The chatter is relaxing and fluid. I have a second helping, and Tom keeps the wine poured. I'm tipsy enough that I ask Tom about my cabin. I hadn't planned it, but I'm so comfortable that it just comes out.

"So, Tom, Carol tells me that there are a lot of rumors about my cabin, none that she believes are true. What do you think about the mystery of the Howards disappearing from town?"

Tom's face changes from jolly to stoic. My heart skips a beat. Carol hardens a bit and interrupts, "Tom, you know they have all these crazy stories about the house being haunted; it's complete absurdity."

I didn't say anything about the house being haunted.

Tom clears his throat. "Yes, it's all absurd, really." The notable transition in his voice has me spooked.

I try again. "Yeah, but the mystery is where the Howards disappeared to, right?"

Carol stands up. "Tom, will you help me clear away these plates? Emily and I have some artwork to discuss in the studio."

Tom looks at Carol and smiles, his facial expression lightening. "Of course, honey."

I feel the need to help, but I'm distracted by the abruptness of the change in topic. I offer, but Carol responds with a fake airiness and asks me to open a bottle of wine and take it to the studio while she helps Tom carry the dishes to the kitchen.

I grab the bottle that Carol hands me and take it to her studio. I'm alone with a wine buzz, a bunch of paintings, paints, and my paranoid mind. From Tom's reaction, it's apparent that he and Carol might not be on the same page about my cabin.

Why is Carol trying to get Tom to hold back information? Why did she mention the house being haunted instead of the Howards disappearing? Tom looked like he saw a ghost.

My nerves are a thing now, so what better way to resolve them than to drink them away. I pour myself a glass and sip quickly. To distract myself from the uneasiness I feel, I find the sketchbook again and turn to the page that Carol mentioned she would tell me about. I sit down in one of the two large chairs on either side of a small table overlooking the lake and wait. Carol comes in and plops down in the other chair. She looks over at me, grabs the bottle of wine, and pours herself another glass.

"Sorry about Tom. He lets the gossip get to him, that's all. It's not a subject he really likes to talk about. He just wishes he could have been here to help the family."

I nod without saying anything. I don't think the truth is going to come from Carol. It's Tom I really need to talk to.

I look out the window to the lake. The sun has just gone down, and there's a pinkish light lingering on the horizon. We sit there in silence, both looking out onto the lake. I feel a calmness that has thankfully replaced any awkwardness between us.

Carol says, "It took me five minutes to decide to buy this cabin after seeing this view. You know, there's just something about it. It's like there's a force that pulls me. I can sit here for hours, and I don't know where the time goes. The lake has a vibration to it that I can't quite discern."

"Maybe it's haunted," I say with a bit of sarcasm and irritation. Carol's face stays serious, and she doesn't respond.

I finish my glass of wine and decide it's time to head out. I thank Carol for dinner, and she invites me to her infamous full moon party the following week. She says everyone lets loose, and she makes sure of it. I promise her I'll be there. Tom waves at me from his chair in front of the TV and I wave back as I leave.

CHAPTER 20:

The morning is spent painting, sketching, and being at peace with the view of the lake. Creativity has never been so fluid for me. Ever. I almost feel as though I'm in a time warp, in some sort of trance, while my hand moves. My mind somehow stays separate. It meditates and relaxes while my body does the doing part. It's being in the present moment with a twitch, like something else is in the room with me. When I finally glance at my watch, I see that I've spent the whole morning painting, and my stomach is talking to me.

I make a quick cream of potato soup, the stacked brochures from the visitor's center catching my eye as I stand at the stove. The top one is for Chimney Rock State Park, and I peruse it as I eat. When I'm done, I put on my tennis shoes. It's time for a hike.

The sunlight angles through the trees, rays of light splitting around the branches. The fresh breeze brings a subtle chill to my skin. I choose a trail that isn't too intense, but one I know will feel like an accomplishment when I complete it.

Many tourists have the same plan for the day. I'm not alone, but I have enough space to think to myself. My thoughts drift to the cabin, the creepiness of how the Howards left town. The cabin has a strong presence to it, more than any other place I've ever been. I ponder how my productivity seems to be heightened like never before. It's more than just being inspired. Is it a haunting? Why would what happened to the Howards seem so scary while what's happening to me is so elevating? At least, for now it's elevating. It could go south.

I round a corner and find a stopping point to look out at the vista. The scenery is vibrant. I'm joined by a young couple. We all just stare straight ahead. Finally the woman says, "Well, that's just breathtaking."

I smile. "Yes. It is." Just as I say it, a gust of wind blows by and pulls the brochure from my hand. It flutters on the wind current, and I try to grab it but miss. The brochure flies in front of the couple; the woman tries to catch it and misses.

The man holds his hand up and snatches it right away. We all laugh as he hands it back to me.

The woman turns to me and asks, "Are you from here or visiting?"

"I'm renting a cabin on the lake for a month. How about you?" I can tell they're visitors, but I ask anyway.

"We're staying in Asheville and took a day trip over to do some hiking. So you're staying here? Wow, are you part of the filming? I didn't think it was possible to rent a place with all that going on."

"Filming? No. Filming for what? I haven't heard or seen anything about it."

The woman stares at me for a second, then smiles. The man gives me an uncomfortable look and signals to the woman to keep going. She waves goodbye, and they leave me with more confusion.

My thoughts are scattered, my mind circling. Everyone is playing a part in my life. Are they all actors? The neighbors are actors who are trying to scare me. What about the cabin? How do they create the sensations I'm feeling in the cabin?

My illusion of reality gets blown up. The thought of everyone keeping things from me strikes my heart like a bullet. I realize that I've gone too far into the depths of my mind about the same time I notice I've strayed from the trail.

I began the hike observing nature and feeling it within me, getting lost inside myself, only to discover I'm now actually lost in the woods on a mountain. I panic. My breathing speeds up. I look at the trail map, but I can't make sense of it because my mind can't focus. I move in a circle, returning to the exact same spot.

My phone. I can call for help. No. There's no cell service. I lean against a tree. *What would Carol do? Climb a tree? Maybe reception will be better.* When I look up, I see someone walking toward me. I call out. The person doesn't respond or change pace. I can't tell anything about them. Is it a child? Boy? Girl? Adult? At first, I think a little girl, but that's not right. Then I think a little boy, but that doesn't seem right either. The person finally stops and stares at me. Fear climbs up my spine. They're the height of a six-year-old with the face of an adult. They have long brown hair with white skin.

It takes a moment to find my voice. "Hi. I'm lost. Do you know your way back to the trail?"

The person ignores my words and walks past me. I follow, staying quiet, and I abruptly find myself back on the trail.

They turn around and say one thing to me. "Your past is here. It follows you like a burden. Only after you turn to face it will you fully be able to live in the present." I watch as they turn around and walk back in the direction we came from, but they never look back.

I run along the path to the end, grateful to see my car waiting for me through the tears in my eyes. I'm relieved I've made it back safely, but I'm exhausted from the stress. The hike didn't clear up any confusion, only added to it. *What kind of production is this life I'm living?*

I need space and don't want to stay inside the cabin when I get back, so I put on my bathing suit and head down the stairs to the lakeside. I spread out my towel on the dock and sit on it while taking in the scenery.

People are outside all around the cove. I see the families to the left and right of me, their kids doing relays back and forth to each other's docks. Two women sit on the dock to my left. I assume they're Leslie and Cynthia. They chat while they watch the kids, yelling out now and then when a child gets out of line.

I lie back and stare up into the sky. The clouds look like brush strokes, sweeping side to side. Interesting. Tree branches border the top of my view, then a yellow butterfly flits past, bouncing in the wind current. I hear distant screams from the kids.

I focus back on the clouds. I could swear I painted the same cloud pattern on my canvas this morning. Spooked, I stare longer. They're exactly the same shapes I put into my painting. Is this real? I blink to clear my head, but the sky still looks the same. I leave my towel behind as I head up the stairs to the porch to look at the canvas. I know I didn't take any hallucinogens. What a grand coincidence. I take a picture of the sky with my phone, then a shot of the painting in its current state. My heart rate quickens. I'm still not certain how this could be. I compare the shots back-to-back on my phone. Questioning my sanity is not a good place to be, a reminder of when my world and reality were turned upside down.

It's early, only one-ish, but I open a bottle of wine anyway. I need it to settle my anxiety. Things have been good; the alcohol won't hurt me. I'm a little ashamed, but I talk myself out of it. I'm on a working vacation, why not have a drink?

Pop. Pour. Sip. Deflect.

I grab the bottle and make my way back to the dock to relax. I stare out onto the water and hear music playing in the distance. The wine does its job to calm my anxiety, and my mind goes back in time.

Sienna was maybe two months old. Kyle had another work trip, and I was alone and vulnerable to my own mind and the heavy responsibility of taking care of a newborn. I'd finally realized that the younger the child, the more the mother needs a team of people. But for this trip, my mother-in-law wasn't available.

I stayed in my pajamas all day and just took care of Sienna. Feeding, changing, bathing, and crying. Repeat. It felt that I wasn't getting anything accomplished. The house was a mess, and I had no desire to clean up. Just taking care of Sienna was enough. It was monotonous and seemed never-ending.

I wondered how those moms who had three-plus kids stayed on top of things. I felt like I was always running behind. Time slowed during the crying sessions, then sped up during naps. Kyle was on a longer-than-normal trip, and I was losing my mind.

Leaving the house had to be calculated and planned. Even with the best plan, nothing went the way it was supposed to go. I got to the point where I stopped leaving the house. I stayed home and did the same thing day after day.

I'd always struggled with routine. I didn't like it, even though I knew it was something good to have. I found out during those early days with Sienna why routine really wasn't my thing. Days started running into one another, and nights into days. I lost track of it all. I was on autopilot. But the life in me changed. My soul had left me, and nobody was home.

Sleeping didn't happen at night. The crying in the middle of the night was the worst. I would get back in bed, the monotony of the caretaking and breast-feeding making me feel trapped. Kyle called me one evening and freaked out. I was mumbling, and he said I wasn't making sense. He cut his trip short and rushed home early.

When Kyle found me, I was on the floor in the kitchen, barely coherent, mumbling about the schedule and repeating what I had to do. Wake up, feed, change her diaper, bathe, repeat. I hadn't showered in a week. When I finally came out of it, I asked him what time it was, and I freaked out because I thought I had left her in her crib for an entire day. But really it was only two hours. She was sound asleep in her crib. I had barely slept at all for a week, and I had crashed on the floor out of exhaustion.

Kyle decided not to travel for a while, and he promised that his mom would always be available to help if he did. He changed after that, became more involved. It changed me too. I lost trust in my ability as a mother.

"Hey... Hey, do you live here?" says a blond girl of maybe seven or eight. She's in the water looking up at me.

I snap back to the present. "Well, I live here for a little while. I'm renting the house for a month. Do you live here?"

"Yes... I live there." She points to the house to the left of mine.

"What's your name?"

"Suzy. Do you like wine?"

I laugh. "Yes, I like wine. How do you know what wine is?"

"My mommy drinks wine, but she won't let me taste it."

"Well, you're a little too young yet. It's for adults."

"Why is it okay for adults to drink and not kids?"

She swims over to the dock, climbs up, and sits down in front of me.

"Well, it has alcohol in it, and that's not good for little people's brains while they're growing."

"Well...I think it's bad for adults too. They act stupid when they drink it."

"You're quite observant, Suzy. I agree with you. We do act stupid."

"So why tell kids to not drink it and then you do?"

"I guess we need to feel something different as adults. Something that gives us an excuse to act with no inhibition because it's not acceptable to be vulnerable and ridiculous."

I realize my words probably shot right over Suzy's head, but she nods as if she understands.

"Aren't you scared staying in that house all by yourself? I heard ghosts live there."

"Really? I heard that too, but I think they're nice ghosts. I've been here for about a week, and I feel safe, all except for the creepy basement."

She wrinkles her nose and laughs. "I never like going down in creepy basements either."

"What have you heard about this house?"

"Oh, the family that lived here all went crazy and left in the middle of the night, and no one knows where they went. And my friend Jessie and her older brother, Joshua, went in the house on a dare and saw a ghost, a woman on the porch painting a picture. He ran out of the house, all freaked out. None of the kids went back after that."

"There you are, Suzy." I hear a woman behind me. She walks up with an annoyed look on her face. "I've been calling you to come back. You're bothering this poor lady." The woman turns to me and says, "Sorry, I hope Suzy is at least being polite."

"She has. It's been nice talking to her."

"I'm Cynthia. We live next door."

She stands over me and blocks the sun. I reach out a hand. "I'm Emily. Nice to meet you."

"Suzy, it's time for lunch. It's yours and Jessie's turn to make the sandwiches for the rest of the kids."

She turns to me. "Leslie is the neighbor on the other side of Carol and Tom's house. She's the one I've been sitting with on the dock. Have you met Tom and Carol?"

"Yes, I had dinner with them last night."

"Oh, I'm not surprised. They're in everyone's business."

She rolls her eyes, and I like that I understand why she does it, even though we just met. To have an inside story before meeting someone feels ahead of the curve. Cynthia seems bouncy and bubbly. We would probably never be friends. However, I want to ask her questions. I want to understand how Leslie and Cynthia co-parent like this and screw each other's husbands.

Is that the secret to surviving this life? To bend the rules and not listen to what society tells you, just make your own? I'm intrigued by how normal Leslie and Cynthia seem. I want to know if they're happy. Whose idea was it? Are they stuck? Do they regret it? Do they fight? Do they feel in control? Does it keep things alive in their marriages? Does it buffer the difficulty of raising kids? Does it work?

I bottle all my unanswered questions up into a smile and wave goodbye as Suzy and Cynthia leave. Cynthia ends with, "I know you're here for some time. I'm right next door if you need anything."

That's interesting. I didn't tell her how long I'd be here. "How do you know that?"

She replies, already walking toward her house, "I know the owner. She told me."

The conversation with Suzy felt good, and yet it made me question the house even more. I'm going to assume there's a chance of a ghost. I wonder whether that ghost has cast its energy on my painting. I shiver at the thought and try to use logic and reason to calm my anxiety. If a ghost is a painter, it must be a good ghost, right? Hopefully.

I want to ask Cynthia more about the owner. Who is she? Who would buy this house with these rumors? Does the owner even know about the stories?

CHAPTER 21:

I had packed a week's worth of clothing and planned to just wash and wear them again. A washer and dryer are available, and it's time to make my way down to the basement and face my fears. Plus, I'm on my last pair of underwear. Daytime is the perfect time to venture down. I plan out the whole process. I'll have my phone with me with the flashlight app on. I need to check if there's detergent available, and if not, I need to buy some.

I'm going to enter from the outside, as it looks less scary. There's a key in the kitchen labeled *basement key* that I'm sure will fit the door by the dock. I debate whether to take Chastain's advice to wear my clothes over again without washing them, but that just seems silly. I didn't want to keep fearing the basement, making up stories, avoiding facing my fears, wondering what's down there. I'm going to face it, leave nothing for my imagination to wonder about.

The windows on the back wall of the basement allow natural light, and I take a quick peek inside at all the clutter and disorganization. The washer and dryer are on the far side, toward the front of the house. I unlock and open the door. A cobweb catches my face as I walk inside, and I pull the sticky web from my hair and ear. I wonder where the spider is. Hopefully the web is old, and the spider has moved on. The stagnant smell hits my nostrils the minute I step inside. I look straight ahead until I reach the washer and dryer, then look around for detergent. I don't see any nearby, and I'm not in the mood to search, so I decide there is none. A trip to the grocery store is due. I hurry out the door and lock it back up, fear not dispelled, anxiety still there. I'm not relieved.

I need to pick up a few other things, so I make a list and head out the door. I bravely make it out of the driveway and point my car toward town. The town grocery store is the only one for miles around. I grab a cart and make my way to the produce section where I see Cynthia and Leslie are shopping together. Cynthia makes eye contact, does a double take, and smiles. We greet each other, and she introduces Leslie, who has a serious look on her face and just a slight smile. She's not bubbly like Cynthia.

Leslie says, "I hear you're renting the house in our cove."

"Yes, I have it for a month. Cynthia told me you know the owner?"

"Cynthia has met her. I haven't. I heard the house is pretty nice on the inside."

"Yes, it's nice."

I'm distracted by something that I can't place about Leslie, but that takes a back seat to what I want to ask Cynthia. "How was the owner of the house? I mean I've heard some rumors about it that would scare off a seller."

Cynthia and Leslie look at each other, and Cynthia responds, "I don't know what you're referring to."

"Suzy told me that the house is haunted, and there are rumors the previous owners disappeared."

Cynthia laughs a little. "Oh, those kids have such imaginations. Don't listen to them."

"Yeah, but I heard it's kind of a known thing. Carol doesn't believe it either, but she knew about it."

Leslie says, "Oh, Carol told you? That's funny. She's the one who believed it the most out of anyone. She even—"

Cynthia interrupts her. "You can't trust what comes out of Carol's mouth. She lives off gossip like nobody's business. Go to her dinners and parties because they're fun, but know that she'll use your life as a good story for her next group."

My lack of guard with Carol now feels wrong. A pit of anxiety in my stomach opens up, and I'm now doubting myself for trusting her. Then I think about the dirt Carol has on them, and I push my concerns away. I change the topic to the house.

"But you said the owner called you, Cynthia. What did she say, and what do you know about her?"

"I don't know her, really. She told me to make sure you felt at home. I guess you're the first guest she's had. She called me before she bought the house to ask some questions about the property, but she never mentioned the previous family."

"But the story Carol told me about the previous owners is concerning, right? And then the rumors."

Cynthia smiles. "Carol just likes to entertain people. We all love her for it, but don't take it to heart. She's got a story about everyone."

Including both of you, I think. What strikes me is that Carol had avoided talking about the cabin at all. She didn't want me to get caught up in it. But I'm getting nowhere with these two, so I change the subject.

"Well...it looks like you have some time without the kiddos to shop."

Cynthia nods. "Yeah, we get our once-a-week grocery shopping done together. Our husbands are watching the kids."

"It's great you're so close to each other and can raise your kids together."

They look at each other with straight faces and then back at me. Leslie says, "Yeah, we kind of planned it that way. It's not easy doing it alone. Cynthia has my back, and I have hers when we need each other."

They give each other another look, and I swear it feels like they know I know their secret. And they're pissed about it. But if they really knew what I think of them, then they'd know I'm not judging them for their values. I'm applauding them for finding ways of staying afloat in this life.

They seem to give each other a signal without words, and Cynthia says, "Well, I have four different types of cereals to gather and ingredients for potlucks galore. We'll see you in the cove." She giggles as they walk away.

They take off, and I grab the rest of the items I need and make my way out. I should take a break from asking about the cabin. It's a dead-end conversation.

CHAPTER 22:

Docks. What rhymes with docks? Clocks, smocks, socks... I make it out early to the dock. The sun is deliciously reflecting off the water. Coffee in hand, I beat the activity in the cove. A glorious ten minutes of solitude sitting in one of the red Adirondack chairs before the silence is invaded by a kayaker gliding through the water with subtle gurgles of water from the paddle swinging from side to side. The indirect company and sounds aren't bothersome, just part of the picture.

The slight chill, the warmth of the sun, and the breeze alleviate a burden I didn't realize I was carrying. I've lost twenty pounds of energetic mental weight. My steps feel lighter, and my arms feel elastic and flexible. I grab the rolled-up towel at my side and lay it out flat on the dock, then lie down and look up at the sky. Purity. If I could bottle up this moment and smell it forever, I would. How can the air be the perfect temperature it is, the sweet smell floating by from nearby blooms? How can the dock rock like it wants to calm me down? How can activity that I don't control, that I'm not logging in to, keep me entertained? I don't want anything right now, and I don't need anything. I'm full of this moment. Why does it feel like it won't last forever? Because that's one thing I know for sure—it won't last. Something will disrupt it, whether intentional or not, negative or positive, cyclical or singular. A nuanced moment will occur, or an unconscious change of mood will set in. Still, I feel the moment, even while fearing it will leave me. Another one will come along and destroy this one. A memory will flash. Something will happen.

I roll over and get to my knees, then push my rear up to the sky as I shift into a downward dog position. My perspective has changed; the world is upside down. It's still a perfect upside-down world. The distant noise is a boat zooming past. I don't see the boat, but the back side of my head does. I see the house, the chairs, and the porch above. Just as I start to turn my head, a small black butterfly flutters past, bouncing in its flight pattern. It lands on the dock, rests its wings, and snares my attention for a few long seconds. Then it pops up and flies over me. I shift to a plank position, look out over the cove, and a breeze hits my face. I watch the butterfly soar on the wind current over the lake. Sunlight reflects a purplish-black hue off its wings.

Switching back to a downward dog position, I focus on the red Adirondack chair. Out of the corner of my eye, I see something move on the porch. I collapse to the dock and twirl my body around to stare at the porch behind me, now in an upright position, catching a clearer view. *What the heck?* My mind tries to be logical. It's a squirrel or something. Must be. But then I see a dark, shadowed movement again. I blink, thinking there's a particle of dust in my eye creating the illusion of something there.

Just as I'm about to get up and go check it out, a noise comes from my left, near Tom and Carol's house. A little boy, about the age of three, skips down the steps to the dock all by himself. His dark hair looks freshly cut, and his red shirt is vibrant against the wooden stairs leading down to their dock. Just ahead of him, a blue kickball bounces down the steps. His laughter echoes through the cove, and his excitement for the chase spills out of him. I'm wondering who he belongs to. Carol and Tom have a granddaughter, not a grandson.

The little boy, gaining speed as he heads toward the dock, holds my attention, and fear for his safety spikes my adrenaline.

Where are his parents? There's an unsupervised child getting close to the water. I watch him, as it looks like he's going to keep going onto the dock at the end of the stairs, but instead he stops and grabs the ball right before it lands on the dock. He looks out to the lake straight ahead of him, turns his head away from me, then peels off back to the house. Never once did he look my way or acknowledge I was there. I switch my attention back to my cabin as I realize I forgot about the shadowed enigma on the porch. Distracted by a more immediate fear, and now this one has lessened.

Carol and Tom need to know there was a little boy who almost plummeted into the lake chasing after a ball. I decide to walk over to their house. I slip on my flip-flops and walk up to their front door and knock, but no one answers.

I'm curious about the boy, so I go around their house and try to find him. I circle a couple of times, but he seems to be gone. I hear a splash; my heart jumps. It's just a duck, landing on the water's surface. I look toward Leslie and Rick's house. I remember Carol stating they have four children. Maybe the boy is one of theirs. I walk over to get a better look, but there's no car in the driveway and no one walking around. Several towels are hanging to dry on the back railing of their deck.

I turn around and look back up toward my cabin. *What about the dark shadow on my porch? Maybe the little boy was playing on the porch before running out.* That's the most logical answer, one that will help me sleep at night, but it doesn't really help now. The logic starts to waver. There's another possibility: the rumors might be real, and the cabin does have strange things happening.

CHAPTER 23:

I'm knocked out of my productive trance by my phone ringing. It's Dr. Nash. Shit. We had an appointment that was supposed to start twenty minutes ago. I answer the phone. "Hi, Dr. Nash. I completely forgot to cancel our appointment. I'm out of town."

"Really? I'm so glad that you could get out of town, but I wish you would have canceled. I'm going to have to charge you for it."

"I know. I'm sorry. The trip pretty much happened overnight."

"Well, since I have you on the phone, we can talk for the rest of the hour."

I don't want to dive into my emotions. I'm enjoying my time being productive, which feels more therapeutic than talking about my shitty past and how it's affecting my current situation.

"So where are you? What's going on?"

"I'm at a cabin in North Carolina for a month. Arin paid for my trip so I can get my work done for our next exhibit—Metamorphosis."

"Well, how the tides have changed. Weren't you in conflict with Arin when we talked last? How did you resolve it?"

"It wasn't really resolved. She dreamed she paid for my trip here and then decided to do it in real life. I let her, so I guess we're good."

"How do you feel about that decision?"

"At first I was annoyed that she thought she could buy her way out of the conflict, but I also played a part in it. I'm here now.

And I'm happy about that decision, so I really don't think about how it came about. I've gotten out of my rut, and I'm painting, so there's that."

"That's great, Emily. How does it feel to be painting again?"

"It feels like I don't need therapy anymore."

Dr. Nash grunts as if she thinks I'm oblivious to the fact that I'm a candidate to stay in therapy for life.

"Good. How are you feeling about Sienna?"

The question feels like a knife slicing through my heart. Distracting my mind from Sienna is what I've been doing. "I've been working on my paintings and exploring the town." I feel a pang of guilt for enjoying myself and not thinking about her. It feels like betrayal. The anxiety starts forming again, and I can feel my heart rate increase.

"Have you talked to Kyle lately? You know it might help you deal with what's going on. You had Sienna together. Perhaps he could be a support to you, even though you're no longer together."

"No, he isn't part of my support system. He hates me. How could he forgive me?"

"Have you tried talking to him? How do you know?"

"He hasn't reached out to me. I can't imagine him forgiving me, and I don't think he should. I'm not worthy of it." I feel shame creeping into my gut.

"Everyone is worthy of forgiveness. If you can tell me some specifics, then I might be able to help you, but you haven't given me much to go by."

"I left my family, okay? I ran out on them thirteen years ago, and that was the biggest mistake of my life. I thought I was saving Sienna, but I wasn't. I thought I was saving her, and instead, I destroyed her."

"Who knows what would have happened? You can't do that to yourself. This is the way it is. You have to accept what has occurred, or you'll suffer and suffer and keep suffering. There comes a time when you need to let it all go. Holding on to the shame doesn't change what happened. In fact, it'll keep what happened alive instead of letting you move forward with your life."

I'm crying. The pain is so intense it's hard to breathe. "I could have prevented it. I could have been there for her. I wasn't."

"You were traumatized by what happened in your community. You left because you couldn't handle it. People deal with things differently; you have to know that there was a valid reason for your actions. But what happened later with Sienna? You can't blame yourself, and you need to look at what resulted from it."

The tears stream down my face. My heart is pounding, and my head is full of pain. "I think this is enough, Dr. Nash. I need to go."

"Okay, but can we schedule an appointment next week and do the session over the phone? I'll charge you half. I just want to be able to check in with you. You seem like you're gaining strength. I don't want to lose this momentum."

I tell her I'll reschedule when I get back in town, because the cabin makes me lose sight of time like it takes charge of my mind. I realize immediately that my words raise a red flag for Dr. Nash because she asks what I mean by that. I correct my mistake by saying it's because I'm on vacation, away from my usual routine, and it's easy to lose track of time. She hesitates but accepts my answer, then reminds me to schedule an appointment when I get back.

I lie down on the couch on the porch and fall into a deep sleep. When I wake, I'm groggy, but I remember my dream. I was at Arin's house, and she was having a big party. Her guests were telling secrets to each other, and they quieted every time I neared. Everyone I walked up to, it was the same response. They stared and went quiet. Same reaction, no matter who. I started talking to a random group of people I didn't know, and they gave exaggerated laughs at my words, as if they were acting. It didn't matter what I said; everything was over-the-top important, but only when I spoke. If I didn't speak, they just stared at me. It was a nightmare.

I try to brush it off, but it leaves an uncomfortable feeling in my gut for the rest of the day.

As nighttime flies in and my depression takes on a life of its own, I decide to not do a damn thing and just go back to sleep. Tomorrow will be a better day. I'm counting on it.

CHAPTER 24:

I wake up. It's a new day. I make a quick pact with myself that I'll do things that make me feel good today. I remember a picturesque stone coffee shop in Chimney Rock bordering the Broad River. Instead of my morning routine of add K-cup, press start, that I've created at the cabin, I venture out to the coffee shop. As Dr. Nash has suggested several times, distraction is my friend in this game called life.

The air is fresh. There's something about the morning hours and the mountain air with the rushing sound of a river that sets the tone for the day. I think I'm headed for a great start.

I find parking across the street from the building with The Village Coffee Shop on the sign above the door. The stand-alone building is a bit out of place, yet not. It has an English countryside feel to it. I walk in, and it's packed. An old basset hound with droopy eyes and a collar that identifies him as Nickel shuffles his way over to me. I bend over to pet him. His job as greeter done, he heads back to the fireplace and lies down on the rug in front of it.

The chatter is hushed, a nice backdrop of white noise. Secrets spoken in whispers between close friends. The crackling of the fire adds to the symphony of noises competing with the steaming and frothing and the coffee presses.

I'm second in line to get a latte. I can't help but absorb the environment, the feeling of walking into a European coffee shop with a high-class southern American feel. A bulletin board covered with flyers announces that Monday nights are town board meetings, Wednesday nights are adult Bible study, and Thursday nights are book club meetings.

The Village doesn't just have coffee. Bottles of alcohol line the shelves on the back wall behind the counter. Chairs along the bar offer places to enjoy drinks to motivate in the morning and drinks to relax at night.

By the fireplace, a white cat bats at Nickel's tail. He doesn't notice. The cat gets braver and attacks the hound's face; still no reaction. Discouraged, the cat walks off and finds a windowsill to rest on. I walk up to the counter and find a chalkboard with seasonal lattes listed. The three choices are Rose, Grass Roots, and Butterfly Tip.

I ask about the grass roots one and go with that. The barista gives me a hard look. She has tattoos that cover both arms. I picture her having a tough Boston accent, but she asks with a sweet southern drawl if my latte is for here or to go. When I say it's for here, she asks where I'll be seated: the valley—which is the floor we're on, the dungeon downstairs, or the treetop upstairs. I tell her I'll be upstairs on the treetop floor.

I make my way to the second floor and sit at a wooden table by the fireplace. One large table occupies the middle of the room, with a few smaller surrounding tables. The back of the building has a floor-to-ceiling window with a clear view of the Broad River and the mountain behind it. A balcony juts out on the back, where several groups of people have congregated, sipping and chatting. A few other tables are filled with couples talking. One couple sits at a table opposite mine, across from the larger one, their voices rising above the hushed chatter.

I struggle to maintain solitude while their conversation invades my thoughts. A few minutes later, a server sets my latte on the table. I want to sit there and just take in the environment, but the voices of the couple across the way invade my meditation. I can't focus on anything but their conversation.

At first it's about his break-up with a recent girlfriend and how it went south. Then it switches to a psychic named Dorothy. How the woman's mother visits her every Sunday, like she's a therapist. The woman went once, and the psychic was correct about a new job that came her way. I have questions about Dorothy, this psychic who seems to be able to read someone's future with accuracy.

The guy asks the questions as if I'm whispering them into his ear. I'm the invisible third wheel to their table. Dorothy has been living in town for five years. She took over the house after her mother passed. I'm intrigued by this woman, yet I've never believed in psychics. I'm pretty sure they're all scammers, and the gift doesn't exist. He asks her where she gives the readings, and it dawns on me that I passed her sign in Lake Lure, en route to Chimney Rock.

The white cat glides up the stairs and weaves between the loud couple's legs. They pause their conversation and pet the cat for a minute, until it wanders off and jumps onto a table to clean itself. The pause apparently inspires them to move on, and they get up and leave. As I finish my latte, I get on my phone and book an appointment with Dorothy, the town psychic. What's the worst that could happen?

Dorothy is sitting on her front porch sipping iced tea as I park and walk to her house. She stands up and introduces herself when I ask if she's the famous psychic.

"I wouldn't call myself famous, but Dorothy the psychic is correct." Her voice is dry and to the point. There's no warmth to her. She's more weathered, like life has put her through many obstacles.

Her presence makes me feel a little sheepish. In retrospect, I'm not sure why I thought a reading from a psychic was a good idea. It's too late now, though. I swallow my fear and tell her I want a reading. I pay her ninety dollars for an hour, the same price as my last therapist who wasn't a doctor. Her face says she isn't messing around, so I decide not to bargain with her.

Dorothy invites me up to her porch. I follow her past two wooden rocking chairs with turquoise-colored seat cushions and a small red side table in the middle with iced tea in a sweaty glass on it. Many pieces of antique furniture crowd the porch, but all items have their place. We stop at a table covered with a cloth that has a moon and star pattern. There's a pile of worn-out cards stacked on one corner of the table, with an ashtray and a lit cigarette at the opposite corner. Two chairs face each other. The porch looks dated, but it's been refreshed with white paint, similar to the back porch of my cabin. It looks as if they were built in the same decade. The cement flooring is painted with a checkerboard pattern of black and white. White candles burn on another table by the front door, which also holds crystals, incense, and a Buddha.

Dorothy directs me to sit down in one chair, and as she sits across from me, I take a good look at her. She has short brown hair with crooked teeth. Her eyes are glossy and small, but they have depth to them.

She settles into her seat and stares at me, her face stoic. It's as if she's gone to another place in her mind. A look crosses her face, like she has just realized something but is confused by it. After a few more seconds, she snaps out of it and looks back up at me.

"This sometimes happens when a tragedy has occurred."

What happens? Does she mean Sienna? Anxiety fills my gut and I ask her, "Is there anything I should know?"

She has a look of deep concentration on her face, then shakes her head a bit, as if coming back to the present. "I don't know right now; nothing is clear. Let's start with a card reading, past, present, and future. The cards have labels, but don't take them literally. Their meaning is for me to decipher."

She shuffles the cards and lays out three in a row, face up. They have a collage of colorful images on them. She points to each card and reads the titles, relating them to each time period in my life.

Dorothy studies the cards and then looks up at me. "Something tragic happened to you that you're not willing to process. Do you know what it is?"

Fear overcomes me like a train ramming into me. I search my memory for something to say, pushing away cobwebs, not wanting to discuss what I did in the past or what happened to Sienna. I finally say, "I left my husband and my daughter. I ran out on them. I regret what I did, and I think my daughter hates me for it. I didn't go far. I mean, I tried to stay in her life. But I couldn't be there for her like she deserved."

Dorothy waits a moment before she replies. "Your husband did love you, but he couldn't bear to see you in pain. It broke his heart, and he felt powerless. Where did the pain come from, Emily?"

My heart beats faster and my palms feel sweaty. I try to think back to when I was married, but my mind sees darkness, negative space, nothing there—a roadblock. Do not enter. "I don't know. I was depressed. I couldn't get out of bed. Postpartum depression. It comes on sometimes after you have a baby. It was awful. I don't want to remember it."

Dorothy looks down at the cards and begins speaking. "You've had tragedy in your life. This card indicates you've suffered alone, but you have people who care about you." She moves to the next card. "This card is for the present; you're at a crossroads. There's opportunity for growth and acceptance of yourself and the past, but you've been stuck and aren't progressing."

Dorothy sits back as if something has just dawned on her. Her eyes grow bigger, and she looks up at me.

Cautiously, she asks, "Who is the woman with long dark hair? Why is she important?"

At that, I gasp and jump to my feet. I have no control over my body or my mouth. "Are you talking about Mei? No, no, no... I don't want to think about it." I shake my head as tears form in my eyes and run down my cheeks. "You can't bring her up. I won't. It's not fair. I'm so sorry, Mei. Oh God, I'm so sorry. I didn't know. I could have been a friend. Then she wouldn't have done it, and we would still have our children."

I trail off as I realize what I've said. I stop talking and sit back down. Dorothy hasn't moved or reacted. She grabs a box of tissues from another table and offers it to me. I take one and wipe my face.

When I've composed myself a bit, she breaks the silence. "I don't like to end on a negative note, and I want you to know that you're capable of healing. You *can* move forward. Your future card has growth and healing all over it, with bright skies at the end. You can get through this. But...this other card represents the darkness that shadows you, and I'm not clear on how everything will play out."

I sit in silence for a moment, taking in her words. "I'm sorry for my reaction. I don't know what came over me."

Dorothy waves her hand at me. "You've been traumatized. But I also feel an interesting exchange, self-healing and Lake Lure."

What the hell does that mean? I'm drowning in my emotions, exhausted and annoyed by how quickly the beauty and promise of the day turned. Being vulnerable to strangers is not a habit of mine.

"Dorothy, thank you. I think it's time for me to go."

"Emily, you know where I live."

No fucking way will I return. I would have run to my car, but the town is small. I don't want to do anything to create gossip, since I still have weeks at the cabin. I push Mei back into my distant memory where she belongs, shoved deep, so I don't have to deal with the pain.

Dorothy watches me as I leave. Questions about the cabin hadn't even come up, the whole reason I went to see her. I don't want to think about my past. I want to know about the cabin's past and why it seems to have a life of its own.

CHAPTER 25:

I used to be able to anticipate a good night when I was young and energetic. I ponder why I used to be like that, and when that gift went away. Probably the weight of life, getting married, being a parent, contributed to it. There were way too many things to think about, worry about, that were more important than sleep. Even after I left my family, I still couldn't get it back. Or maybe I'm not worthy of it. Days are filled with anxiety and guilt; I don't walk through life with purpose and confidence anymore. A delayed response to the current situation.

I don't want to foresee anything. Everything feels out of my reach. But being at the cabin has been a drastic change, and I find my gift has returned. I know this night will be fulfilling. There's excitement again, anxiousness that feels comforting instead of alienating.

I made one of my favorite dishes to bring over, an herbed black bean salad that people have liked before. I look in the mirror, and I'm not horrified at what is looking back at me. The woman in the mirror deserves some recognition for tonight.

Carol has invited a younger group of millennials who come and hang out on the weekends at their parents' houses on the lake. She said they aren't married and usually just want to have a good time. She thought I might get along with them, particularly a woman named Jessica. I might be able to let loose and live out some carefree moments with her. "Jessica is smart," she told me earlier today. "You'll like her. She's brilliant in her attitude and just kind of skirts around everyone with her happiness."

Sounds like a pill I'd like to take.

I grab my dish and head out the door. As planned, I was somewhat late. I hate the anticipation of waiting for people to show up. At an hour past the start time, all the early arrivals should be buzzed.

I walk outside, and the music hits my ears. A crowd of people are hanging out on Carol and Tom's dock. The laughter roars, and I hear one lady's high-pitched laugh above them all. Cynthia. I smile. I can deal with unhinged people. Unlike Arin, they probably won't pick up on my semi-depressive energetic force.

I don't bother knocking on the front door, and it's pure chaos inside. The music here is different from the dock music. Blondie is blaring, and everyone is dancing. I know no one. I walk through the crowd of people, the recipient of multiple curious glances as I search for a spot on the island to set my dish.

The energy in here is off the charts. Carol spots me from where she's dancing with a young woman wearing platforms, and she heads in my direction, the young woman following her. "Why are you so late? You've missed Gary doing a keg stand."

The young woman wraps her arm around Carol. "Next full moon party, we're getting a live band, right?"

Carol rolls her eyes. "I still have to make sure our dock can handle that much weight. Remember what happened to the Kenskys a few summers ago?"

The young woman shakes her head. "No, have it on the lawn in the back."

Carol looks back at me. "I'm being rude. This is Rachel. She lives on the other side of the lake."

Rachel reaches out a hand. "Carol is my second mom. And the best partier I know."

Carol laughs. "Got to get it in while I'm still young and beautiful!" She grabs my hands. "Let's get you a martini, and then you have people to meet."

She pulls me through the crowd, music blaring. Tom is standing in the corner with a group of men laughing about something. We get to a bar where a server is making martinis.

I scream to Carol, "You didn't tell me this was such a big event."

Carol says, "What?"

I don't repeat myself, just wave her off, and take the drink the bartender hands me. We make our way outside to the dock. Leslie and Cynthia are drinking with their husbands.

A bunch of people are jumping together to the music in a corner. Carol goes over to them. "Okay kids, settle down. I want you to have fun, but I also want everyone to live another day. Don't let the full moon be the death of you."

Carol turns to me and grabs my free hand to pull me into the dance. I would usually be shy with such a crowd around, but no one seems to give a damn about what anyone's doing. I find myself smiling and dancing, not caring what I look like.

The music rolls, and so does the night. The dancing keeps going. Carol keeps handing me martinis until I'm beyond drunk.

Let's talk about vodka drunk compared to wine drunk. They aren't the same. Vodka drunk feels as though someone captured my brain and numbed it from the inside. It's not fun. The music is slowing, and my movements follow. Carol is doing her rounds, and she comes back to me with a beautiful woman in tow, introducing her as Jessica.

Jessica is tall and slender with long, flowing brown hair and green eyes. She flashes a gorgeous smile, and instead of shaking my hand or hugging me, she kisses me on the mouth, then pulls back and looks at me. "Hi. I hear you're the mysterious new painter on our lake. I must know all about you. Have you met Terry yet?"

"No."

"Oh, please come with me. He's going to love you."

She grabs my hand and drags me to another spot on the dock where a vivacious group of people are talking. They all get huge smiles on their faces as Jessica walks up. A few of them say in unison, "Jeessss...what's up?"

She introduces me to the group, and as I'm trying to remember everyone's name, I catch her mouthing to them, "She's renting next door." Their eyes get big. and I'm suddenly the hit of the party.

I feel like I've gone back in time to my childhood. The next thing I know, we've settled into a serious conversation about the education system and how it sucks that most people can't afford it. Everyone's going into debt over it, and it's all the government's fault. I shake my head because, at this point, I can barely follow the conversation. I agree with most of what they're saying, but the conversation is going too fast for my thoughts to keep up or me to contribute.

Jessica says, "That's why I'm getting involved with an organization that challenges the current education system. It doesn't make sense anymore. It hasn't changed in over half a century, and it's no longer compatible with today's children. It forces them into holes that kids no longer fit in. And then higher education...ugh."

Another guy says, "If we didn't have rich parents who paid for everything, we wouldn't be here hanging out every weekend on a dock."

A woman chimes in, "This country is going to shit, and who's going to save..."

I miss the rest of her question as Jessica turns to me. "Emily, what do you think about the education system when it comes to art? If art dies, what will become of this country? Our creatives keep us living, right?"

Everyone turns, and suddenly all eyes are on me. I'm numb, can't think of a response. Quiet stares. Shit, I can't form a thought. "Art is life," is all I can get out.

They stay quiet for a moment, and then Jessica says, "Yeah. You kill creativity, you kill the ability to live and find purpose in life." Jeez...what did I walk into?

Jessica pulls me away from them to a quieter corner. "You're so pretty, and you're shit drunk."

I laugh. "You're pretty too. It's cool when someone pretty notices another who is pretty."

She laughs. "Let me catch up with you, my new friend. See you later tonight. Don't get lost in the woods. There are bears out there." She leaves me swaying by myself.

It's time to find a bathroom. I go inside, and it looks like everyone in the house is in line. My next best option is the patch of woods between Carol's house and my rental. I laugh to myself about the bear comment. I find a place that seems secluded and free of people, and I'm about to go when I hear a familiar voice coming from the bushes not far from me. There's also a man's voice, and they seem to be having a serious conversation. I don't mean to eavesdrop, but they'll hear me if I get up to leave.

The man says, "I'm so tired of this. Why don't we just get divorces and stop living the lie? I love you, and I can't stand to live separate from you."

The woman says, "Rick, are you serious? Our spouses are not normal human beings. Our lives will turn to shit. Our arrangement will be ruined. It works for the kids, and it works for us."

"So do you even love me like I love you?"

"Be practical. It won't work; they'll destroy everything we've created."

"He's not worth your time for one minute. He's a piece of shit who doesn't deserve you."

"I know that. But there are more important things to consider than my absolute happiness, and I don't know if I'd be happy on the other side."

They're quiet for a moment. "Leslie, I love you, and I'll do anything for you. But we both have to be on the same page. I'll keep quiet for now, but I think it's best to tell them how we really feel about each other. I mean, we didn't see this coming, did we?"

I remain quiet, but I swear I haven't had to pee this urgently in my entire life. They finally leave, and I pee a river.

I stumble out of the woods and make my way back to the dock. After I'm there, I wonder too late why I didn't just go to my cabin to pee. I laugh out loud. There are lots of people but no familiar faces. I expect to see Cynthia and Leslie with their husbands, but they aren't anywhere to be found. I go through the house and see Carol is in a conversation with a group of people. I'm not the best conversationalist, so I turn to head back to the cabin. Time to call it a night.

I get to my house and grab a bottle of water from the fridge. I'm heading for bed when I hear a knock at the door. I open it to Jessica and two of the people she introduced me to earlier.

They all shout in unison, "Emily, can we come in? Pleeeeaaase." They laugh and walk in before I can answer.

Terry says, "Oh shit, I've been dying to check out this cabin forever."

Jessica looks around. "Right? It's so awesome you got this fucking cabin." All three of them are staring like it's one of the seven wonders of the world. I sober up a little and try to be a good hostess.

"Do y'all want some water, wine?"

"Yes!" they say. "Water!"

"Do you guys always speak like that?"

"No!" they all say in unison again, and we all laugh.

Jessica asks if they can go out to the porch, and I lead everyone outside. They inspect the porch like they're hoping to find something. Anna and Terry smile at my painting. Everyone plops down on the couch, and Terry takes out what looks like a joint. "Mind if we smoke?"

"I don't care."

Terry offers me a hit, and I accept it. There's a progression from drunk to high, and it seems to happen fast. The vodka drunk is no longer headlining my world, and it's like my senses wake up. My thoughts were diluted from the alcohol, and now I'm wide awake, but I focus on things I usually wouldn't.

Terry's laugh seems to be the loudest, and I can anticipate when he'll laugh next. Jessica's words are coming out faster than the movement of her lips. The other chick, Anna, is making exaggerated movements. At one point, they look over at me and start laughing. I can't remember when I've seen so much energy bouncing off people. It's as if they can read each other's minds and know how to respond to each other. There's no awkwardness in their interactions, no pauses, hiding one's thoughts. Everything is said out loud. I'm not paying attention to their words, though. I focus on their actions.

I drift, and my eyes become heavy. At first, it's messy, this dream I'm having. Flashes of different people in my life, scrolling of a sort, then bam. Definition. I'm in the cabin, and I can't seem to leave. Every exit, the door is locked. I'm stuck inside. I try to go to the porch, but the porch door stays locked. People pass by, but they don't notice I'm there. I scream, but they don't hear me. I pound on the doors, but they don't notice I'm there. I run through every room in the house trying to bust out a window, but the windows won't break. I avoid going down the stairs to the basement for what seems like a long time. I don't want to go down there. Maybe that's the way out—go down and face it, and then I can get out. I walk down the steps and open the door to find Mei standing there with a knife in her hands, blood dripping off it, a crazed look in her eyes. I scream.

I awake to Jessica standing over me shaking my shoulder. "Em, are you okay? You passed out, and I think you were having a wicked dream. You were screaming."

My eyes focus, and she blinks. "Say something so I know you're with us."

Anna says, "What do you mean 'with us,' Jess? She's not possessed."

"You never know in this cabin, Anna. You never know what it does."

Terry is laughing in the background. His laughter is contagious, and Anna laughs with him. They both start screaming, mocking my scream.

Jessica gives them a look and they shut up.

"I'm fine. You're right. I had a bad dream. The mix of alcohol and pot...um."

"Wait, let me take one more hit before you tell me about your dream," Terry says, giggling.

I'm not as annoyed as I should be at these people. Their vibe is light, and I want to laugh at myself along with Terry, but I can't.

Jessica seems relieved that I'm okay, and then she laughs too. "My God, you scared me. This cabin! Don't you feel it, y'all? Everything is intensified by a hundred."

Still laughing, Terry looks at her. "It is. I'm sorry. If I could stop laughing, I'd try to figure out how this cabin is so sick."

Jessica looks at Terry and Anna. "It's time guys. We need to sober up and let Emily go to bed."

Terry shakes his head. "No. I'm not doing it this time."

"Yes, you are."

They look at each other and suddenly head off the porch, running toward the lake.

Jessica calls back, "Come on Em, we're jumping in the lake."

I walk down after them as they all dive in with their clothes on. I watch as they dunk each other in the water, screaming. Jessica gets out and comes over to me, pulling my arm.

"If you think about it, you won't do it. Just come in. It'll help tomorrow, I promise."

I walk in a few steps and dive in. The water rushes over me as I submerge myself. The cold washes over me, the sensation intense. I pop up, and they're all on the shore.

Jessica calls out, "I've got towels in my car."

Anna responds, "Only you, Jess. Who travels with towels in their car at all times?"

I follow them to where she parked her car. They all dry off as best they can and climb inside. Jessica lowers her window and smiles. "Brunch tomorrow."

Without waiting for a response, she speeds off.

I turn back to the cabin, more than ready for bed. There's a figure moving around on the porch. I blink and rub my eyes. She's no longer there. I know everyone left. I saw them get in Jessica's car. I call out, "Hello," then feel stupid for saying it. No one is there. It's all in my head. I walk over to the porch, and there she is, sitting in the chair. Her face is impassive, absent. I freeze.

CHAPTER 26:

At first I'm terrified. But then I realize Mei doesn't know I'm there. Her face is droopy and sad. She stands up and walks right past me. I can't move. I know it's not really Mei. I know it. But she's here with me, nevertheless. She walks around the cabin as if she's in some sort of a daze. She paces back and forth, mumbling to herself, looking down at the floor. Maybe if she looked up she would see me, but it's as if she plays the same scene out over and over. Pacing, worried, mumbling. I wonder what would happen if I stand up and get in her way, but I'm frozen. I can't talk, and I can't move. I'm afraid if I make a change, it might produce another outcome, a scary outcome. My heart is pounding, and I'm trying my hardest to keep my breathing even so I don't interrupt what she's doing. I sit and watch as she paces. I felt fucked up before, but I'm totally sober now, even though I know I can't possibly feel anything normal.

I watch the pattern of her steps to see if her feet land on the same spot every time. If her movements are exactly the same, she could be a hologram. But I can't focus. It seems the same, but my brain won't allow me to track her. I'm too anxious.

I wonder how long this will last. Will I have to watch her until the sun rises? I don't plan on going to sleep while she's here. I want to devise a plan, but I don't know the rules for this situation. If I move, what will happen? If she notices me, what will happen? I'm too scared to test any of my theories. All I can do is watch her.

The watch on my wrist helps me keep track of time. Thirty minutes go by, and I can't stay awake any longer. I feel the sleepiness creeping up, and my brain starts to shut down. I doze off, leaning back against the door. I don't know for how long, but I snap back to Mei. I keep my eyes wide open and watch her. She walks back and forth in front of me over and over. She comes so close to me, but I don't feel a rush of air as she moves past.

Finally, she does something different. She pauses at the top of the stairs that lead to the basement, then takes clumsy steps down the stairs. When she's halfway down, I move forward so I can still see her. By the time I get to the stairs, she's all the way down and has paused at the door to the basement. She opens the door and steps inside.

I exhale like I'd been holding my breath for an hour. The relief is intense. For what seems like an eternity, I watch the door to the basement to see if it opens. Should I go down and see if it's locked? My nervous system is shot. I can't do it. If she comes back through that door while I'm checking it, I'll lose it.

I'll sleep in the chair on the porch. It feels safer. I have more options for escape, and I won't feel trapped like I would in the bedroom. I don't want to go sleep in the bed with the door closed and then open it in the morning to find her on the other side. No place feels safe at this point. The chair will have to do.

I grab a throw. The feeling of Mei's presence creeps through my body. It's heavy with sadness. I don't want to go there, but my mind does anyway. I feel a hot tear burning down my face, and the next thing I know, I'm out.

CHAPTER 27:

I wake with a start, sure I only slept about twenty minutes, but the sun is shining in my face as if it's midmorning. Waking up is like coming out of a coma. There's no gentle transition. I'm unconscious, and then I'm awake and aware. My head is pounding as I stumble to the kitchen to make coffee. I take a sip and head back to the chair.

My phone rings. It's Jessica. Her voice sounds chipper, like she didn't drink or smoke last night. Something about brunch with a couple of other folks. She's talking, but my brain is lagging. I don't manage to get a word out, just muttering on my end. She laughs and says, "Okay, so brunch at Rainbow Tavern at 11:30, got it?"

"Yes, got it."

I don't know why I just agreed. I don't ever remember being so hungover before. Then it hits me. Mei. The cabin feels different now, as though it's been violated. Like it's no longer safe.

Jessica said the Rainbow Tavern has the best drinks to cure hangovers. I look at my phone and see it's 9:30. I've got some time to get my shit together before I head over.

I take a long shower, throw on some clothes, and head out the door. The restaurant is in Chimney Rock, right on the river. The day is beautiful, and it seems everyone in town has the same idea as Jessica. Half the people I see were at Carol's house last night. Many of them smile at me in acknowledgment. I'm edgy, my thoughts choppy from the hangover. My brain can't keep up with the movement of my head. I find Jessica, Terry, Anna, and some other guy whose name I can't remember sitting at a table on the back deck overlooking the river, the rushing sound of the water supplying the background music.

For a while, I just listen to them talk, laugh when they say something funny. But I don't feel part of the conversation. They're nice, and they do their best to include me, but I have no desire to take an active part. I enjoy being halfway involved, listening to the river behind me, eating. We sit there for a while, and I order a few of the hangover drinks. I'm already feeling better and more in tune. My mind starts waking up and becoming more alert. I look down to the river at the large rocks with people on them.

Jessica follows my gaze. "Oh, we're going down there today. Do you see the rock all the way over there with the multicolored paint on it?" She points to a rock on the other side of the river. "That's my favorite rock."

She pauses, then says, "So how are you feeling? You seemed like you were hurting a little earlier."

"Yeah, I didn't get much sleep last night."

I don't tell Jessica about the ghost of Mei or whatever it was I saw. It almost feels like it never happened. The whole incident feels surreal and distant.

"You brought your bathing suit like I asked, right?"

"I did."

"This is a gorgeous day to be on the river. It'll cure your hangover right up."

My mind wanders, and moments later everyone is gathering their things and getting up. I missed the plan for what's next, but I follow along. We take off for our cars to grab our suits while Terry buys beer. We girls all pile into the restaurant bathroom to put on our suits. I get mine on, then head out to put my purse in my car. As I'm locking the door, I look across the street and see Leslie walking alone into Burntshirt Winery with a book in hand.

I watch her for a second, but she doesn't see me, so I head out to meet up with the crew behind the tavern.

Like in a beer commercial, everyone runs toward the river in their bathing suits looking happy and fresh. Jessica leads the way to her favorite rock. She dives in, and we all laugh and splash each other as we follow her. It's a bit of a swim to the other side of the river, and I fall behind everyone else, going at a slow pace. The cold water is burning my skin. I wade through rapids and rocks and finally make it to the big, flat painted rock.

Terry hands me a beer. "Here's your prize for making it."

I laugh and take it. The new guy seems to be into Jessica. He's attentive and touchy. Terry sits next to me. He smiles. I can judge men's smiles, and I'm pretty sure I know what he's thinking.

"So Jess told me you're a painter, and you're working on your next exhibit."

I smile and return his flirtatious eye contact, because that's what I do best.

"Yes, I have an exhibit coming up."

These times are exciting, the first interactions, figuring out if he wants me or not, reading the stares and the body language. Until this trip, moments like this were the only highlights I had. At least after I lost Sienna.

He leans back on the rock while I stay sitting up.

"I'm sorry I was such a stoner last night—laughing at fucked-up things. Jess was so mad at me. It was kind of scary hearing you scream. How is that cabin treating you? I still can't believe we were hanging out there. I've been dying to see inside it for years, and at the same time scared shitless to go inside."

After Mei's visitation last night, I choose my words carefully.

"It's been different. I'm productive with my painting, and I feel renewed, but I also feel like there's something else there."

"I heard something very interesting about your cabin."

"What?"

"Apparently kids dare each other to run into the house. They said they see a naked woman who looks like a goddess painting on an easel. When she sees you, she stops and poses on the couch on the porch, like she's the subject of the painting."

I laugh because I know what he's doing.

"Really?" I turn back to look at him.

"Yeah, and you know what?"

"No, let me guess. I look just like her."

He laughs. "How did you know?"

I roll my eyes. "I've heard the story before."

"Wow, look at you knowing the dirt of the town. There's some other dirt that I bet you don't know, though."

"Like what?"

"Ummm...should I tell you? Nahhh..."

I don't like games like this, but he's cute, so I let it slide. "You're mean. We just met, and look how you're treating me."

"Do you know what people say about you in town?"

I couldn't possibly imagine. They don't know me, and I've only been here a week. "What?"

Instead of telling me anything, he sits up and kisses me. I kiss him back because his execution worked. I like the connection. There's a force between us, and I feel a rush in my stomach that's similar to the water running in the river. I expect him to ask me to go back to my place or his, but he surprises me.

"Come on, let's get in the water." He stands up and reaches out his hand, but everything goes quiet, and he says, "Mei isn't going away. She'll be back, and Michael too."

My heart stops and my brain sputters. I stand up and look at him. "What did you just say?"

He looks at me, confused. "I said Anna and Jess are coming back... Are you okay?"

I shake my head, stuck in a memory I don't want to be in, confused. I know he said what he said. What the hell? His gaze turns concerned, but before either of us can say anything else, Jess and Anna climb out of the water to join us.

I can't really see any way to bounce back, and I'm sure my face shows my confusion. Jess looks at me, and then she looks at Terry. "Oh my God, what did you do, Terry?"

She turns to me. "He's such a sleaze." Then back to Terry, "What did you do?"

She pushes him like he's a naughty little boy. He doesn't say anything, just turns to look at me to see my reaction. I need to save face. This situation is on me. I need to find a way to resolve the awkwardness. I blame me, my head, my thinking for what I thought I heard. I'm not in my right mind.

How would he know about Mei or Michael? How would he know that I saw Mei last night? How would he know that she would come again? How would he even know the names Mei and Michael? All eyes on me. Fuck.

I let out the most natural laugh I can muster. "Terry's a sweetheart!"

Jess looks at him, smiles, then turns to me and whispers like no one else can hear, "I knew he would fall for you."

I laugh again, and though it sounds fake to me, it seems real enough to them. Nothing comes of it. The awkwardness is forgotten.

We frolic and splash in the river for a couple of hours before I use my art as an excuse and tell them my painting is calling me or some shit like that. They all hug me before I leave, and I love it.

CHAPTER 28:

When I reach my car, I towel off a bit and put my clothes on over my swimsuit. A knot forms in my stomach. It's amazing what can distract your mind from your own concerns.

As I drive back, the flapping of wings in my gut is intense. I have to stop the car to breathe and figure things out. I pull into a restaurant parking lot in front of the lake and try to sort out what's happening to me. The people here are nice, and I'm productive at the cabin. I feel inspired. The cabin is perfect. But Mei.

The silly notions I'd dismissed about the house being haunted now seem real. I won't let my mind go down these corridors. I must maintain my sanity. What bothers me more than anything is that I can't get a straight answer out of anyone about the cabin. Everyone refers to it as this anomaly, a place everyone wants to experience, but not for too long. I don't know whether to run home or just laugh out loud. The absurdity of this situation is annoying. I tell myself I need to keep a level head. If Mei comes back, I'll confront her, because it's all in my head. I need to go toward the fear, not run away from it.

I'm about to get back on the road when a police car pulls up next to me. He lowers his window, and I lower mine as well. "Hi," I say.

"How's the cabin treating you?" He smiles big. This makes the third time I've been asked that question today. My nerves spike. Are these people for real?

I respond with a distant, "Good." But I wonder if I should have told him what was really happening. He says bye and drives off. Now what? Everyone is driving me crazy. As I drive back to the cabin, I do my best to convince myself that it's all in my head.

CHAPTER 29:

I open the door thinking I'm going to walk into some bizarre scene, but it's just the cabin. Quiet and still. I walk around a bit, and for some unexplained reason I feel better, calmer than before. My anxiety is soothed, and the fluttering inside my gut feels more like excitement. I have the urge to paint again. Like magic, my fear is gone. Not only do I feel safe, but everything makes sense again. I grab a canvas and paint. Hours roll by, and they are beyond productive, my arm moving with fluidity, like an internal rhythm has taken over. My paintings have an edge, almost like an invisible muse is zapping me with creativity and opening a new door to my intellect that I didn't know was there. My strokes feel choreographed. My mind doesn't know what's next, yet my hand does. The fear of Mei has left me.

My arm tires, and when I stop painting, I realize I'm starving. I look in the refrigerator and see the bean salad I took to the full moon party, half eaten. Funny, I don't remember bringing it back. I brush the thought off. I was drunk, no surprise. I eat a big bowl of it, and I can feel my body translating the food in my belly into energy.

I go back to my canvas. The scene I was painting has mountains and a big sun rising from the water. I look at it for a moment; it's happy and bright. But what's that? I didn't intend to paint that. As if I have binoculars for eyes, I zero in on it until I can't unsee it.

Hidden within the sun and the rainbow are images of ropes that appear from a distance to be flames or embers of the sun and texture in the rainbow. The effect jolts me because I didn't have the awareness that I was putting them there. Further, ropes are a thing in my life. I feel the need to sit with it. Interesting. I find myself in a flashback.

Sienna is fifteen, and I just got home. I grab my phone that I'd accidentally left behind and find a text from Kyle.

You need to come to the police station, Sienna was taken.

My heart drops to the floor. Powerless is an understatement. I text her and call her, but no answer.

The image flashes out, and I'm left with the memory. Sitting alone with it. My heart is heavy, and my mind is shot. Sadness climbs through every vein in my body.

I find myself curled up on the floor by the chair, staring at the canvas in front of me. It's dark outside. I have no concept of time. I catch movement inside the house in the corner of my eye. It's Mei, only she seems to be in better spirits today. She's doing something in the kitchen and humming to herself. I hear the clanking of things being shoved and tossed around. The noises are rhythmic and delicate. Then Michael runs up from the basement. The rush of joy when I see his smiling face is something I never expected to feel again. I want to run over and swoop him up and hold him forever.

He runs around the stair post to Mei, and she turns and gathers him up, gives him a big hug, and holds him tight. They stay there for a long time, and I revel in the big smile on my face and how elated I feel to see them together. My heart feels full, and I fall asleep.

CHAPTER 30:

I wake up to my phone ringing. I'm in bed, but I don't remember how I got there. I answer, disoriented. "Hey, Chas."

"Hey, Em. I'm just checking on ya. I see you haven't gone down to the basement yet because you answered." Her laugh seems too loud and a bit off. I'm quiet.

"Em, are you still there?"

"Yes, sorry. I haven't been sleeping well." I need to figure out a way to spruce the conversation up, so I change my tune. "I've been partying with some people I met here. They're fun."

"Great! Have you...um...met anyone?" She releases a giggle.

"Well..."

She busts out laughing. "I know my girl! You're gettin' it, aren't ya? Spill it. Tell me everything."

"Chas, you didn't even let me finish. It's just a guy, and we kissed, that's all."

I stumble to the kitchen to get some coffee. I feel like a log hit my head.

"Umm...more to come, I'm sure. Keep me clued in to the next episode. Where will this kiss go?"

I'm not in the mood to laugh with Chas. She's great at keeping me energized, but I'm not feeling it. I do my best to fake some positive energy because I don't want her to detect that anything is wrong with me. "I will definitely tell you."

"I can get away to come visit for a weekend. I'll be able to make it out the last weekend you're there. Just to confirm, the cabin isn't haunted, right? My time away from my family is sacred. I'm not in the mood to die or be haunted."

"No, it's not haunted." I hope she can't hear how fake my laugh is. It's true, though. I don't think the cabin is haunted. In fact, I feel like I'm the one who is haunted, and maybe Chas being here will help.

"You haven't heard banjos from the townspeople?"

"No, and I think you'd love the people here. I already know some of their dirty laundry."

"Oh, these people actually tell you shit? Like they're for real about themselves?"

I laugh. "I don't really think they want to be. I think I hit the gossip jackpot by staying next door to someone who knows about everybody's business."

"Good, it keeps things spicy."

"Chas, I'm thrilled you're coming." I want to say that I really need her here, but I know that'll flag concern. "I can't wait for you to be able to relax and hang out. I'm happy you're coming, and you're doing it for you."

"Yes, I can't wait. I've gotta go. The kids are screaming for breakfast. Love you."

"Love you too. Bye."

I hang up and hold on to the feeling of relief. Chastain is coming. I need her. I feel like I'm losing something of myself. Or maybe I'm discovering something. Either way, I feel strange. I need my old friend to give me a sense of reality, to make the hallucinations of my past go away. The fact that Mei and Michael have shown up brings on a feeling of uneasiness that cuts deep. The feelings around them are something I don't want to rediscover. I have a hunch that they'll keep coming back, though. It's an out-of-control feeling, like even if I ran, Mei and Michael would find me. They won't just go away.

I drink my coffee in silence, and I try to change my mood. I need to get through this morning and turn it around. I go outside on the dock to get some fresh air. I hear children laughing and look around to see where they are, but I can't tell where the sound is coming from. It stops, but I still see no children.

It feels eerie out here. I can only see glimpses of the mountains, as fog lingers and wafts about. The fresh air is nice, but this overcast morning doesn't help me feel better, just adds to my anxiety. I go back to the cabin to get another cup of coffee. Maybe another dose of caffeine will change what I'm feeling.

After I get the second cup, I head back outside, and I see Tom walking over to his car. I wave, and he waves back. I change direction to go talk to him.

"Hi, Tom. How are you?"

"Good, I'm just headed out to meet some friends to play golf. How are you doing?"

"Doing okay this morning." I hold up my coffee cup. "Trying to get more of this in my system."

"I hear ya."

"So I wanted to ask you some questions about the cabin."

"What about it?" He looks concerned.

"I really want to know what happened to the family that used to live here. I think Carol knows more about them than she's told me, and I assume you would know too."

His face takes on an expression like he's trying to think of something, but he can't quite recall the details. I think he's faking it.

"I don't know anything else."

"I heard the family went crazy before they left abruptly. What did Carol find out about them? I know she knows something. What happened to them? I need to know."

"She did search for the family, but I don't know what she found."

"Did she figure out where they lived?"

"Yes, I'm pretty sure she did, but I don't know if she reached out to them. She might have called them."

"What did she find out?"

"I don't know, Emily. I don't pay attention to half the things she says about people. I can't keep track."

I can tell he's just trying to skirt around the conversation. "So do you think Carol has their number?"

"Maybe she still has it. You need to ask Carol directly. What about contacting the rental company?"

"That's a good idea. I hadn't thought about that."

It's a dead-end conversation, but he gave me a good idea.

CHAPTER 31:

The rental company isn't far from the cabin. The building is off the main drag going into the town.

I walk in and see a young woman sitting at a desk in the front. She smiles and welcomes me. Before I came inside, I sat in the car while I tried to think of a reason to contact the rental company, and it dawned on me that I hadn't told them about my little visitor, the mouse.

"How can I help you?"

"Hi. I'm renting a cabin, Hidden Joy, and I wanted to let you know that I saw a mouse on the stovetop."

The woman crinkles her nose. "I'm sorry to hear that. We'll take care of it. With these older homes, it's hard to keep those little suckers away. I'll let our pest control company know. I can contact you when they go out to the property. Is there anything else I can do for you?"

"Yes, I actually have a couple of questions about the cabin."

"Okay, go ahead."

"So the reason I chose this cabin is because of its history. I stayed in Lake Lure a year ago and heard all the stories going around about it. I was so excited to see that it was offered as a rental. Have you been here long enough to know about it being haunted?"

She gets an excited look on her face, and she leans forward over the desk. "You know, I told the owners they should advertise that it's haunted. It would likely triple the revenue. I know there are so many freaks out there who would want to stay in a haunted cabin."

Her eyes open wide. as if to say, *oh no I just offended a guest*. "I didn't mean freaks. I just would never pay money to stay in a haunted cabin. I couldn't sleep at night, ya know? Not my idea of a great vacation."

She laughs. I can tell she's scrambling to cover up her slip.

"No worries. I know it's weird. Really, I want to get more information about the family who lived there. Every time I visit a place, I like to learn the backstory. This is different. The ghost stories aren't promoted like the other places I've stayed. Do you know what happened to the Howards?"

"All I know is that their house is haunted, and they all went crazy and left town."

"You don't know anything else about the family before that happened?"

"They seemed like a normal, quiet family, and then, snap."

"I mean, how did the story unfold? How did everyone find out what happened?"

"Well...the kids didn't want to go home. They started going over to friends' houses. These friends started telling their parents. The town started to talk. The friends' families still live here. That's really why I thought we should make this house a legit ghost property, but the owner thought it would scare people away."

"Do you know some of these people?"

"Sure. One of them owns the house right next to the cabin."

"Who?"

"Cynthia and Rick Jenson. Have you met them?"

"Yes, but I didn't know they lived there when the Howards did. Do you have any information on the owner of the house? Like can I contact them?"

"That's a good question. Most of the owners prefer to be anonymous and have us handle the rentals, but I can see if they're willing to be contacted."

She types on the computer for a minute. "The owner isn't listed in the system, but there's a signed contract somewhere in our files. Can you believe they still have paper files? Electronic filing is another thing I suggested, but no one listens to me. I need to get approval from my boss to give you their contact info. I can get back to you about that and the pest control. Will that work?"

"Yes, it will. Thank you."

"Before you go, I have one question. Have you seen any ghosts? Have you seen the painter?"

I consider for a moment what I want to tell her. I lie. "No, I haven't, but that mouse really had me going."

She laughs out loud. "I bet."

She stares at me for an awkward moment, and it makes me think that the "I bet" was more sarcastic than agreeable. She continues, "Talk to you soon."

I walk out with a knot in my gut. My next stop will be Cynthia and Rick's house.

CHAPTER 32:

I pull into the driveway of the cabin. Just as I park, I see a text from Jessica.

Hey friend, what's up? Terry can't stop talking about you. Lol. Want to meet up Thursday night? I'm having a thing at my house.

I consider how I feel about it. It will give me some space from the cabin. Which I need. I text her back.

Love to. Let me know details.

I park, but instead of entering my cabin, I walk over to Cynthia's house. She smiles when she sees me at the door. "Hi, Emily. What can I do for you?"

"Hi. I'm sorry to bother you, but I'm dying to know more about my cabin and its history."

Cynthia giggles. "Why? Is it haunted, really?"

Her response is loud and seems out of character even for her, exaggerated. I wonder if she's drunk.

I respond, "Um...well."

"Oh my God, it is." She laughs. "Are you freaking out or what? Have you seen the ghost, the naked painter? No way! Tell me everything."

Her reaction makes my tentative belief in the ghosts I've seen seem silly, laughable, and no big deal. My guts have been twisted, and my emotions flip. Her laugh lingers on and slows down. If I had a paintbrush, I'd add water to tone down the brightness of her color.

I attempt to appease her. "No, I haven't seen any yet. Some interesting things have definitely been happening, but I can't be sure it's the cabin."

She laughs again like my comment is absurd. "Oh, it's the cabin all right. Are you ready to leave? You can stay here. We have a finished basement."

I wonder why she's changed her tune. She and Leslie said the stories were just rumors. Now she's shifting her story.

"No, thank you. I heard you lived here at the same time the Howards did. What do you know about them? What happened?"

Cynthia laughs again, and I brace myself.

"Karen ran over here in the middle of the night in this strange nightgown that looked like it was from the baroque era or something. Weird! She woke me up out of a deep sleep. Oh Lord, I could not get back to sleep that night."

"What happened?"

"She said there was a dead man in the basement. When Rick and I went over there, everyone was accounted for in her house, and there was no dead man to be found. I still remember the look on the kids' faces. Two months later, they left town. They probably lived in that house for less than a year."

"What else happened?"

"Karen wouldn't make eye contact with me, and neither would Fred, after that night. They kept to themselves, but rumors were going around that they were losing it, and their kids were always trying to get out of the house and sleep at their friends' homes."

"What were the Howards like before this happened?"

"Oh, they were normal people. I got along with them both."

"Was there anything you thought was out of place about them?"

"Not...really. Oh, wait. Karen had a much older daughter from another father, like sixteen years old, who didn't live with them. That stood out to me. Like why didn't she live with the mother? So weird, and I never saw this daughter come around."

That made me want to know more. "Did you ask her why?"

"I didn't know her well enough to ask, and I guess she didn't feel comfortable enough to tell me. But it felt like there was something there that wasn't good. Of course, I don't think she meant for me to know about her in the first place. The father called Karen while she was at my house one day. She said a few things and then went outside to finish the call. When she came back inside, I asked her if it was Fred, if her kids were okay, because I could tell she was talking about a child. That's when she told me."

"How old were her kids at that time?"

"Around nine and eleven, I believe."

"What do you really think happened to the Howards?"

"They lost their minds."

I wonder if the same thing will happen to me. I wish I'd known about the house before I rented it. Nothing is making real sense.

She smiles big, and it sweeps across her face in a large way, distorting the image. Just then, Suzy joins us. "Mommy, I'm hungry. Can I have a cupcake?"

The exaggerated expression snaps back to normal at her daughter's voice. It stays normal as she looks at me. "That's my cue. I need to get back to dinner."

"One more question. Why did you and Leslie make it sound like the rumors weren't true, and now you've changed your story?"

Cynthia's face turns serious, her voice stern. "I don't know, Emily. Aren't you here on vacation? Just renting a cabin? Why do you find the need to ask personal questions about the people who live here when it's none of your business?"

That's the most serious I've heard Cynthia. My instincts tell me to leave. I turn and head back to my cabin—to a place where I don't know what to expect.

I'm spooked by the conversation. What if they did all go insane? The cabin is feeling more of a place of vulnerability than a place of rest. I pause outside the front door. I could just leave. I could jump in my car and speed off and never look back. I've done it before—run. It seems immature and stupid, considering everything I've been through with my family. I can't keep running from my fear like I did with Sienna. As much as I don't want to be in the cabin, I can't leave. I can't run out on my demons. Giving up never did anything for me except make me feel disempowered and wrong. I walk inside the cabin, this time knowing I'm walking into something that's not only unknown, but could be terrifying.

CHAPTER 33:

I go inside, but my mind is racing. The overcast weather adds to my uneasiness. The edginess pushes me back out the door and into my car. I'm halfway to the town of Lake Lure when I remember the police officer I'd met the day I arrived. I'll go to the police station and ask the officer what he knows about the cabin.

I park down the block, and the walk to the station feels somehow familiar, but my consciousness hasn't yet caught on. There's a female clerk at the front behind protective glass. I start to ask if the officer is available to talk to me when I realize I don't actually know his name. I do my best to describe him, and I see a moment of clarity wash over the clerk's face.

"Oh, you mean Officer Roberts. He's not here, but let me see where he is."

She looks at her computer and then makes a call. She says some things to him that I can't hear, then looks up at me. "He's on his way back to the station, but it'll probably take him at least thirty minutes to get here if nothing happens. Do you want to wait?"

"Yes, I'll wait."

"Okay. You can have a seat over there."

She points to a waiting area, and I walk over and sit down. I have no idea what I'm going to ask the officer. I think of questions like: What did you know about the Howards? Are the stories true? Did something bad happen there? Why did they leave, and what happened to them? I think he'll be able to fill in gaps and give me a comprehensive picture. I type the questions into my phone as I wait. The station seems overly quiet and boring.

The clerk presses a button to talk into the speaker. "He should be here soon."

I nod back in acknowledgment.

The silence is nerve-racking. The last time I was in a police station was the most horrifying experience I ever had. My mind travels back to that moment, and the wings in my gut charge up full force. A sharp pang slices through me.

I walk fast, my breath coming in pants. I'd been holding up well, but as I move into the police station, my tears start falling. I walk through the door and am directed back to the office of Detective Kenneth. Sienna's already there, a blanket wrapped around her, Laura's arm around her shoulder, Kyle standing next to her. A jealous pang runs through my heart. Sienna doesn't look up. She's crying as she answers the detective's questions. My relief to see her alive is unreal. I sit down and try to communicate my support. Laura's disapproval is obvious from the look she sends me. I try to make eye contact with Sienna.

I ask her how she's doing, but the question and my tone don't match the moment, and I feel like an outsider. Laura is taking my spot, a spot that isn't big enough for both of us. She gives me a bitchy look, and it's like I can read her mind. *You're never here, so here I am, filling the void.* The guilt penetrates my heart, and my crying escalates. But my sorrow is nothing to Sienna's, so I try to stop it. It doesn't work. My heart is broken.

The detective asks, "How was it you were alone at the soccer fields?"

In a shaky voice, she says, "My mom was supposed to pick me up after soccer practice."

She gives me a look that is forever ingrained in my soul. Her anger burns right through me. She'll never forgive me for not picking her up on time.

"I kept texting and calling her, but no answer."

I try to explain. "I left my phone at home when I went to pick her up. I went to the wrong location. I thought she was practicing at school and not for her academy soccer league."

I look over at Kyle, and he stares down in disappointment.

"I figured out halfway to the fields that I left my phone at home, but I was sure that was where she was practicing, so I kept going. When I got to the school, no one was there. The lady in the office said she didn't have practice that day, so I rushed home to get my phone."

Sienna, tears streaming down her face, says, "I can never count on you; you're never there when I need you."

The words sting because it's something I've accused myself of as well, but this made it official. I couldn't argue about who I was to Sienna or the type of mother I'd become to her.

The detective says, "Tell us what happened next. What time was it?"

Sienna sniffles. "I waited there, and everyone had left." She pauses and tears again start streaming down her face, but she manages to gather herself together. "It was nine at night. One of my teammates who has a car asked if I needed a ride, but I refused it because I hadn't seen my mom in a while, and I didn't want to hurt her feelings."

The comment punches me in the stomach. The guilt lingers like a bee that won't go away.

She continues. "An SUV pulled up, and a man rolled down the window and asked me where a soccer field was."

Detective Kenneth asks, "What color was the SUV?"

Sienna pauses and wipes her tears from her face. "I dunno. It was a dark color, maybe black."

The detective writes it down, then motions for Sienna to continue.

"I walked up to his car because I couldn't hear what he was saying. When I got up to the window, another man jumped out and grabbed me and pulled me into the car. They tied my hands and taped my mouth." Sienna stops, and I can see how her mind is replaying the events. Then she continues. "I kicked with my legs, and then he blindfolded me, and I felt a sharp pain in my leg, and I passed out.

"Why did you pass out?"

"I think...I think they drugged me."

"Okay, what happened next?"

"I woke up. My hands were still tied. They put tape on my mouth, and I was still blindfolded."

"Can you describe what happened afterward?"

"It was so dark. I was terrified. When I woke up, I knew I had to get away. I was able to get out of the rope because..."

She cries harder. "Because I can escape from being tied up. It's a fucked-up game my friend and I play. We tie each other up and try to escape from wherever we put each other. In the dark. I win every time."

I look over at Kyle, and he's smiling.

"What happened next?"

"I tore the tape off my mouth and took off the blindfold, but it was still dark. I felt around the room and tried to figure out where I was. There were a bunch of other girls in the room."

"Were any of them conscious?"

"No, none of them were awake. I mean, maybe. I don't know."

I can't help myself. "Oh my God, you were so brave."

Sienna looks at me. "Yeah, Mom. I was real fucking brave because I had to be. You left me there by myself to get kidnapped, and then I had to save myself."

Kyle says, "Sienna, it's a miracle you escaped, and we thank God you did, but your mom doesn't deserve that."

Laura looks at Kyle. "Oh, come on, Kyle, are you serious? Sienna is right. Emily wasn't there, and she didn't do anything to help the situation. I'm the one who's always there for Sienna."

Kyle looks down without speaking.

If I could have crawled into a hole and covered myself up, I would have. Laura *has* been there for Sienna. I don't like her, but she's been Sienna's constant. I want to thank her, and I have before, but she hates me the same way Sienna hates me. The weight of sadness on my heart is indescribable. The tears burn as they roll down my face. The detective looks at me. Kyle doesn't say anything.

Sienna spits out, "You look pathetic, Mom. Why are you crying? Do you feel sorry for yourself? I don't feel bad for you. Not only do you look pathetic, but you're weak. You're the weakest person I've ever met in my entire life."

I look at Sienna, then at Laura. Her eyes burn through me. I look at Kyle. He has his head down. I look at the detective with desperation. "Can I leave? I need to be excused."

He shakes his head. "I know there's something else going on here, but I need you to stay so I can get everyone's statements."

I nod in agreement.

Sienna adds, "Yeah, Mom. Go run, go hide. That's what you know how to do best."

I sit there, my face swollen from crying when I need to be strong, but everything she says about me is correct. I am weak, and she is strong.

Laura looks at the detective. "She ran out on Kyle and Sienna when Sienna was three. That's what Sienna's referring to."

Thanks, Laura, I think to myself. *I'm sure the detective needs that bit of information.*

"Sienna, what happened next?"

"I found the door, but it was locked. I knew they would come back, and I tried to think of different scenarios and what I should do. I didn't think of what did happen."

"What did happen?"

"I flattened myself behind three girls who were passed out, and

I waited." Her voice rises almost to a yell, her face red from crying. "A man opened the door, and as soon as it opened, a girl rose in front of him. She blocked me. He kicked her in the face, but I was able to run out the door. He grabbed my arm, and I felt a knife at my neck. He scratched me with it. Piece of shit."

I gasp as Sienna shows the scratch on her neck to the detective.

"I kicked him like he was a soccer opponent I wanted to get back at, and I ran like I've never run before."

Kyle, with tears in his eyes, smiles at her.

"I didn't know where I was, but at least I was outside, not stuck in that room. It was dark. I kept running and running through the woods. I finally found a road and chased down a car. They let me call my dad, and here I am."

She exhales and buries her face in her hands, her whole body shaking. "What about those other girls? Did you find them?"

The detective shakes his head. "We were able to find the location they were holding you, but they'd already left. In these situations, they move fast when someone escapes, so they can't be tracked."

Laura asks, "What have you found so far? I mean, with today's technology, you should have found them by now, right?"

"We're doing everything we can to find out who took Sienna. It's not a rookie, not a loner, but likely an organized group. Sienna got very lucky."

Kyle asks, "How do we know they won't come to take her again? How do we stay safe moving forward?"

"We'll have officers on rotating shifts watching you and your family, but they're not likely to come back."

"How long does that go on?"

"Until we don't feel your family is in any more danger. We'll get into that more later, but now we need to find out everything that happened. You mentioned earlier that Sienna felt like she was being followed. Tell me more about that."

I swallow the hurt that runs through my body and exhale as I begin speaking. "Sienna has been telling me for a year or so that she's being followed, but she made it sound like it was delusions."

"What do you mean delusions?"

"She wasn't sleeping at night. She told me that Laura and Kyle knew about it, but they disregarded it."

Laura jumps in. "Um, excuse me, we did take it seriously. She started seeing her therapist again, right Kyle?"

Sienna looks over to Laura with an expression I can't read, but it says something to me.

Kyle replies. "Yes, we took her to the therapist because of several things that were going on. She started having issues with friends, didn't want to be friends with them anymore. She had emotional outbursts, her attitude became worse, and she stopped sleeping. We didn't know what was going on."

The detective asked, "Did you take her seriously when she said someone was following her?"

I respond before Kyle or Laura can say anything. "I did. I talked to Laura, and she was frustrated, but I got it. Sienna had other issues going on. Also, she didn't have any proof—they were just feelings, but I was concerned. I finally called Kyle and talked to him about it, and he said they were on it."

The detective makes a face like he's not sure how to proceed. "Sienna, why did you think you were being followed?"

She hunches her shoulders. "They were strong feelings. At one point, I looked out my window and swore I saw a man looking in, but my therapist told me I was hallucinating because of lack of sleep."

"Did anything happen that gave you a clear indication you were being followed, other than a hunch, delusions, or feelings?"

"There were a couple of occasions when strangers stared at me in a weird way, but I don't know. I thought I was going crazy."

"Okay. Is there anything else I need to know?"

I'm knocked out of my memory by the clerk's voice. "He got held up. Some young speed racer was going too fast around a curve and hit a tree. He's gonna be a while. Do you still want to wait?"

"No, I'm good. I'll come back some other time."

I leave with the anxiety of the world in my gut and zero information about what's going on at the cabin. I pull away from the police station, but instead of going left to the cabin, I turn right to visit Dorothy.

CHAPTER 34:

Dorothy walks out of her front door just as I'm pulling into her driveway. I wave as I get out of my car.

"Hi, Emily. I knew I'd see you again. How are you?"

How am I? I'm fed up with the half-answers that I'm getting from everyone. Nobody will give me straight answers. And then there are the seemingly unexplainable things that have been happening at the cabin.

I'm sure she can see the frustration I'm feeling. "I might appear unhinged right now, but I really need answers. I feel like you're the best one to ask, that you might believe me."

She leads me to the table we used last time I was here. "Is it time for you to tell me about Mei?"

I hadn't thought she would bring that up. My plan was to get the answers I need, not spill my guts. "No, I actually need answers from you."

"About what?"

"About my cabin. What happened to the Howards? What happened in that house? Why does everything seem so weird? Why does the cabin seem haunted, and why do I see Mei and Michael there?" The frustration brings tears to my eyes, yet it's such a relief to ask the questions out loud.

Dorothy exhales. "Okay. That's a lot to unpack. Your mind is jittery and bouncing around. Are you eating? Are you sleeping?"

"Dorothy, if I wanted a therapist to tell me I need to sleep, eat, take my meds, and journal, then I would have gone to a fucking therapist. I'm coming to you, the psychic, to tell me why my life is a complete tragedy."

Dorothy looks annoyed. "Is your life a complete tragedy, Emily? Really?"

I think for a second. "Yes. My life is a stream of events, and my story beats to the tune of a tragedy."

"I'm not going to offer you reading suggestions because I know you won't read them, but have you ever thought about the balance of life?"

"What do you mean?"

Dorothy's face says she's losing her patience with me. "Life isn't meant to be all good or all bad, and our perception of good and bad is opinion-based and fleeting. At one moment it can mean one thing, another something else, and it'll have yet another meaning to other people."

"Are you saying what happened to me isn't really a tragedy? That I should just look at it differently?" I don't think she's a very good psychic. If she could really read what happened, then she'd change her opinion.

"I'm saying your life isn't over yet. You can look at what you call bad things as opportunities. You're not dead."

Dorothy stares at me. I think for a minute but don't have a chance to respond.

"You can either stand there in front of me and cry about your life or do something about it and make changes. You must accept what you cannot change, then figure out how you can move forward to live the best life you can."

"But my life is shittier than most."

"But my life is shittier than most." Dorothy mocks me, sounding annoyed. "The shittier the better. 'Thank you, Higher Powers, for thinking that I could survive such atrocities. Is there anything else you would like for me to endure?' Say it. You're letting the drought get to you. You have the answers inside.

You're pissing me off with your damn pity party. Grow up!"

Dorothy stands up, walks to the other side of the porch, and lights a cigarette, inhaling deeply.

I don't know how to respond.

She lets out a puff of smoke. "You'd smoke too if you worked for the NYPD. You should also listen to me because I worked for the NYPD, and this is my advice to you. You're alive; make the best out of it. Let the demons of your past be the demons that set you free. Stop making them chase you around. Look at them and do something."

I'm confused. "You were a detective for the NYPD?"

"No. I did exactly what I do now. I was a consulting psychic. I helped solve cases..."

I sit back, surprised.

"What? Now I have some credibility?"

"I mean, yes." I'm afraid to say anything else, but I want to make one more point.

Dorothy interrupts me before I can say anything else. "You can't accomplish anything by weeping and feeling sorry for yourself. Nothing. You have two choices: You can either mope around"—she makes a mocking sad face—"or you can decide to participate and do something about it."

"Okay."

Dorothy rolls her eyes and takes another long puff of the cigarette then sits down, seemingly exhausted. "Okay, now run along. You're stressing me out, and I don't need my blood pressure to rise."

CHAPTER 35:

I collapse on the couch at the cabin. The interaction with Dorothy lends itself to introspection and a theme that I haven't wanted to consider. The fact is, I can't see past myself. My pattern is to run and cry about it. I'm not the lead actress in my own life; instead, I'm the antagonist to my own story. This realization for once doesn't bring me to my knees in grief. It hardens me. With the awareness of my own shortcomings, I realize something external to me. More than one truth can exist at the same time.

The ability to embrace new experiences can be exciting and make us feel brave, but it doesn't mean we have the tools to handle them. There are so many things we let into our lives, unknowing what's in store for us. If we knew what we were in for, would we still be willing to experience them? I wouldn't.

If I knew that I was going to experience motherhood the way I did, I would have made different choices in life. It pains me to think it, but it's true. On the most troubling days, it takes my breath away. It's an emotional punch in the gut. I wonder why everything is geared toward protecting the child, not to protect the mother, who has such a profound influence on the child. The point is lost. If the mother isn't protected, then how can the mother protect the child?

If a mother does what the culture says she should do—just does what she's supposed to do—she's doing it right. No credit is given because it's expected. If she doesn't, or if she's incapable, she's shunned. But still, it's up to her to find the resources to survive a journey that has no right answers.

Why is something that is precious and important to everyone's human development not a priority? Why is it valued and an expectation for women to do it right? I never felt more alone in my life than I did when I became a mother.

My spirit burned out, and I was innocently unaware. I became something foreign to myself. While my spirit died, my soul scrambled, trying to figure out what was happening to my light. My laughter lost its substance and depth. Sadness replaced happiness and vibrated there for longer than was needed. Confusion about who I was supposed to be ran circles around my gut, never settling on something that looked like me. There seemed to be no cure. Art lost its passion. I was a spiritless mother. How are you supposed to produce art, even look at yourself in the mirror, after failing at motherhood?

Maybe there should be a discipline in psychology called motherhood. Or maybe not. Stop it, discipline of psychology. Shut up. I'm tired of you telling me what I need to do to raise the perfect child. You give me the information but never teach me how to execute it in the world we live in today. Are you fucking with me? Are you part of the problem? Are you corrupted too? When can we be honest with ourselves?

I'm a mother, and I've been told my entire life that a mother is the most important person in a child's life, but all I've found motherhood to be is a comparison game of who can do it better. There's a whole lot of pressure, responsibility, resources, opinions, and judgments, but not a lot of understanding.

My child was exceptional in every way. I was shocked by her brilliance and beauty, but I hadn't the slightest idea of how to handle her brilliance in the environment we were living in. She grew at the speed of light, while I chased behind her, trying to protect her and give her the best I could. But she always ran faster. I never quite caught up, never felt satisfied that I'd given her something she could use. My pursuit felt pointless. Not only that, but a threat to her well-being.

I'm numb. My productivity is gone. I'm sitting on the porch looking out into nothing. I'm not seeing a thing.

A power or force of some sort takes over my mind. I'm not in control of it. The lights flick on, and music starts to play. It's Vivaldi. I recognize the rhythm, the dramatic starts, the moments of calmness, only to heighten with another dramatic climb. I know nothing about music other than that I can submerse myself inside it and feel its emotion.

I listened to Vivaldi when I was pregnant with Sienna. Some expert at the time recommended listening to music. Better yet, listening to classical music. "Your child will be a genius at birth." That research was later debunked as just a marketing ploy. However, I believe it was true. Sienna was a genius to me.

Vivaldi's music is the tune of Sienna. He didn't know that one day his music would be the beat to my daughter's existence.

While pregnant, I bought a box set of classical music for my car's CD player. I listened to them all. Vivaldi hit me, and I later realized that Sienna played to the beat of Vivaldi as her life's music. Moments of dance, with lightness transitioning to another intense emotion. Perhaps Vivaldi represents how I feel about Sienna rather than the playlist of her life.

Where's the music coming from? I comb every inch of the cabin, but I don't see anything that can produce music connected to the lights. My stomach turns, and my anxiety heightens. My heart rate increases, and my digestive system starts gurgling, but my mind slows, can't perform the way I want it to.

I look outside, and it's gloomy. The sun is going down, and I'm not sure where the day has gone. The view outside the window doesn't look as beautiful as it did before. It looks edgy and hard.

I don't want to leave the cabin. There is an eerie, strange comfort here, like an addiction. At first, it's great; everything is fun and joyful. Then you need the thing, and it's no longer fun. You need the thing you're addicted to so you can survive the day. I need the cabin so I can survive the day. It feels like the cabin is pumping my heart for me, and without it, my heart would stop. Like if I walked out the front door, I'd collapse and die without the oxygen it's giving me.

I look up at the sky, and the cloudiness cascades through my mind in its pursuit of confusion. I get the urge to go down to the basement. I'm convinced the music is coming from down there. It must be. Where else? I haven't explored down there, just did my laundry as quick as possible. Maybe it's time. But it's getting dark. I need to make sure I can see. I turn off the light, and the sound of Vivaldi is gone. I turn the light back on, and it starts again. I make my way downstairs with Vivaldi lighting my way.

The raw scent of the house awakens my nostrils as I move down the stairs. Its age is revealed, and perhaps its purpose. Vivaldi gets louder and more intense as I walk. I open the door, and the scene isn't what I expect. It's not a basement, but something else. A scene from a movie or something from back in the day. I must go toward it and figure out what it is. I give in to the urge and move forward, and the door slams behind me.

There's a group of violinists playing Vivaldi in a corner, while people walk around dressed in clothes from the baroque era. Everyone is making their way over to sit in the seats in front of the violinists. I take a seat in the back.

As I listen to the music, it pulsates through every blood vessel in my body. I focus on one young girl playing the violin. Her bow is playing my heart. The dramatic ensemble crescendos, and tears start pouring from not only my eyes, but from my entire body. My clothing is soaked through from this display of emotion. The verse slows, and my tears diminish. The moisture dries up, but the sadness lingers. I watch the young girl and listen to the harmony with more intensity. They play for what seems like hours.

The audience responds at appropriate times. The end of one emotional verse is the start of something familiar. When the concert ends, the musicians stand, and I see the girl is dressed in a white baroque-style nightgown. We all applaud the amazing display of talent. She bows with a straight, serious look on her face. I catch a glimpse of her heart, red and beating out of her chest under her nightgown. She stares back at me.

I blink, and there's nothing but a dark basement. The only light is in a corner on the opposite wall from me, tucked away, ever so slight, but bright in the surrounding dimness. I find myself creeping toward it, then I lie on the floor in front of it, alone. I feel scared, but more sad. Alone and vulnerable. But I still feel the strange addiction I have to the house.

My thoughts are filled with Sienna. My heart sinks inside me. I lie there with no more tears to cry. There's nothing left inside me. But there's something about the dry feeling. There's a counter to it. Strength sparks from nowhere. Something twinges inside me, and a rearrangement of a sort occurs. Sitting here in a rank basement next to a small light, I gain an ounce of strength.

I'm knocked out of my musings by the sound of a child crying. I see nothing in front of me, because I'm sitting next to the dimmest of lights. There. In the distance. A small light is moving around. The crying appears to be coming from the direction of the light. It gets closer. The anticipation gets to me. I don't know what I'm about to encounter. The light comes toward me, and suddenly Michael is in front of me. He stops and looks down, still crying. He sits down in front of me. I'm both scared and concerned as I watch him cry. But there's a sense of relief too. He's not threatening. I need to console him.

I hug him, and he lets me. A sense of relief courses through me. I have nothing to say. His fate has already played out, his life taken early. It's obvious his soul can't rest. Why else would he be here?

He looks up. "I'm here because of you. My soul can't rest because of you. Not because of me."

I'm shocked. I didn't think he was even aware of me. "Michael, what do you mean?"

Before he can respond, I see another light in the distance, and my insides twist. Something feels wrong about this light. Something in the air tells me this light is not all right.

He doesn't respond, just stares at me, anger taking over his face. The emotions I feel toward him and the energy in the room shift. I look up, and there is Mei. She's angry too. She stands still as a statue, and she has a shocked look on her face. She's pale, and her hair is plastered to one side of her face.

She looks at me as if I stole her son from her and I should give him back. My heart rate peaks, and I don't feel safe with these apparitions staring at me in anger. A long, dull pain shoots through my neck, and my mouth gets dry. I should try to talk to Mei.

"If you want Michael, you can have him. I miss him too, you know."

She hisses at me. "He's here because of you."

I'm getting worried. "What do you mean, Mei? I didn't bring him here. I didn't..." I can't finish the sentence. I can't say it out loud.

She responds, "Say it. Say what you want to say."

"I didn't... I didn't kill him, Mei."

Her face changes to sadness, and she drops to the floor. I was afraid of this. That's why I didn't want to say it. She looks up and screams at the top of her lungs.

I wake up while she's mid-scream, and I'm in my bed in the cabin. I don't know how I got there. My feet hurt, and when I look at them, the bottoms are dirty. The pain down my neck burns into my upper back. I don't feel rested. My head hurts, full of thoughts, theories, and connections. My eyes ache from lack of sleep.

CHAPTER 36:

I find myself sitting on the porch couch. Instead of taking in the scenery, I'm in my head, and my thoughts consume me. I keep seeing things from the past, images, going round and round in my head. I'm trying to solve all the mysteries. I come up with multiple theories for why things are happening.

Carol is hiding. She knows more, and I wonder whether the Howards are all tucked away in an insane asylum somewhere.

The police officer knows something, and he's corrupt and possessed by the demon from the cabin that's keeping me here.

Cynthia is crazy, and all the people in the cove know my past and what's going on with me. They feel sorry for me.

This is all a big production for a movie, and I'm at the center of the storyline.

My thoughts circle and circle as I come up with new theories. I don't know what's true.

I feel a weight on my body, as if the air inside the cabin is heavy and pressing down on me. It's so much I can't move. I'm frozen.

My phone rings, and I find myself able to reach for it. It's Jessica. "Hey, have you gotten my texts? I've been trying to reach you all day. What's going on?"

I look down and see a bunch of missed texts. "I'm sorry. I lost track of time."

"Well, are you still coming to my house tonight?"

I don't want to move from the porch. I feel stuck there, like I wouldn't have the energy to get up anyway. A pain shoots down the left side of my neck again.

"Jess, I don't think I want to go anywhere. I'm not feeling well. I've got this pain in my neck."

"You've got a pain in your neck? Nope, that's not a good enough excuse. Right, Anna? Does pain in your neck ever work with me?"

I hear Anna in the background. "Nope, it's never worked."

"I don't think I can move from this couch."

She laughs. "Just so happens, we're driving by your cabin. We'll pick you up."

She's not leaving me much choice. "Okay."

Her car pulls into the driveway, and the doors slam. I make an attempt to leave the couch to greet them, but I can't. I feel heavy, like I'm weighted down. They knock on the door and just walk in, then head to the porch. Jess and Anna burst into laughter when they see me.

"Get off the couch, Em!"

I laugh to play it off, but I feel stuck. It doesn't make sense, and I'm trying not to freak out about it. They walk over and grab my arms. There's a tiny resistance, and then it's like I come loose from something. They stumble back and fall on the floor laughing, and my smile turns real.

"We've set you free from the couch. Now grab a dress and put it on. I have makeup at my house. My friend is deejaying. Get your butt in gear."

I follow Jess's instructions, and we head out the door.

We can hear the music all the way out in the driveway. Everyone is dancing in her living room to old-fashioned reggae records. The lighting is a red strobe. The atmosphere is retro. There are probably about twenty people. Jess introduces me to a couple of them in the kitchen while she puts the beer away in the fridge. She turns to me. "We've got shrooms. Want to do them with me?"

"Like the psychedelic kind?"

"No, the portabella kind. Yes, of course, the psychedelic kind."

It feels great to be out of the cabin, but my head is still a bit wacky, and I'm afraid to push it. I know better than to add more layers to whatever's going on with me. "No, I think I'll pass, thanks."

"Are you sure?"

I'm positive. She hands me a beer and pops the shrooms in her mouth. Then she smiles, grabs the beer out of my hand to chase them down, and hands it back to me. "Cheers. Let's go dance."

The floor is filled with people. The beat of the music is a backdrop, keeping the energy up and the beat steady.

The music keeps playing, and my brain is numb. Hours roll by as Jessica and I dance. She feels the shrooms and dances around me in circles. She leaves my frame of reference and then comes back. It makes me dizzy.

My head is spinning, and the air is breathing around me. The sound of the music goes far away and back again. Jess keeps spinning around and around. She stops and looks again at me. She waves her arms around my head and says, "You're in it."

"In what?"

"The cabin. It's got you."

The strobe light casts cycling shadows on her face, and I feel as though I'm the one spinning around in circles.

Her eyes get big, and she smiles. "Are you freaking the fuck out or what?"

I don't know how to respond or what I could say under the circumstances, so I smile. Then it dawns on me. "Did you give me shrooms? I feel messed up."

"I told you. The cabin has you under its control." Her face gets serious, and she says, "There's nothing you can do now."

"Why would you say that?"

Her laugh is wicked. "Because everyone who lives here knows. Don't you get it?"

"What happened to the Howards?"

She points her fingers and rolls them in circles beside her head to signify they went crazy, which just annoys me. "Why are you saying this? Why didn't someone tell me?"

She keeps laughing. "We told you. Everyone told you. You didn't want to believe it. It's sacred ground, man. This whole fucking lake is sacred. We all know it, but that cabin is something else."

"Am I in danger?"

"Are you in danger? That I don't know. Maybe not, if you can keep your head together. But don't worry, I'll break you out of the hospital if they admit you."

She moves closer to me. "Or maybe you're stuck in a movie you can't get out of." She looks directly into my eyes, and a cruel smirk appears on her face.

I'm spooked and annoyed. I turn to walk away, but I'm walking sideways, as if I were the one spinning around and dizzy. I need to get out of here. I find the doors leading to her deck. Fresh air. I catch myself on the back of a chair and sit down. There are several people hanging out. They look at me, then turn their backs. Okay, can't stay here then.

I make my way down to the dock and sit there alone. The night feels different, like it's all fake. Jessica's last statement intrudes on my thoughts, but before I can process it, I hear something behind me, and Terry sits down beside me.

"Hey, how are you?"

"Feeling messed up right now."

"Let the shrooms settle in. Don't fight the feeling and relax. You'll be fine."

"I didn't take shrooms."

He gives me a look as if I'm lying.

He puts his arm around me. "Are you having fun?"

Before I can answer, he leans over and starts kissing me. I feel his hands grab my breasts and slowly make their way up to my shoulders, then to my collar bone and around my neck. The intensity of the kiss heightens, and he presses harder on my neck. I get dizzy, and he presses harder. I open my eyes, and he's staring at me, eyes wide, a crazed look on his face. Suddenly he's pressing with incredible force, choking me. I jerk out of his hold, coughing hard.

Just as I catch my breath enough to scream at Terry, Anna rushes over. "Terry, come quick. Jess thinks she's a fucking butterfly."

Terry looks at me without saying anything, then looks at Anna and smiles. "Well, she is a butterfly."

She laughs. "No, you don't understand. She's plotting a way to make wings so when the sun rises everyone will jump from the deck and float down. She's got a team of people figuring out a way to make them. Everyone has lost their minds."

Terry laughs. "I've got to check this shit out." He looks back at me and asks, "Are you okay? I got a weird vibe from you while we were kissing."

Was the whole choking thing all in my head? I shake my head but tell him I'm fine. He pauses, as if wondering if I'm telling the truth, and then leaves with Anna.

I sit there looking out onto the open water. What just happened? There are no clouds in sight, just bright stars twinkling. I close my eyes for a moment.

I wake up in the cabin. I don't remember how I got there. The pain in my neck is back. I roll out of bed and realize I'm still in my dress. Everything is damp, as if I swam across the lake back to the cabin. Coffee. I need coffee.

Once I have a cup in my hand, I begin to remember the night before, but I don't know if it's a dream or if it really happened. Images come to me in slow motion: people cutting fabric and sewing things together, another group making things out of tinfoil that look like wings, and others making elaborate goggles. Everyone serious, as if they're working at NASA, coming up with some cutting-edge transportation device. Then the images switch to about ten men and women dressed in butterfly costumes with wings made of tinfoil on cardboard and embellished goggles. They all stand on the side of the railing of the upper deck, Jess in the middle with the most elaborate outfit. She stands up straight and spreads her arms out to show her wingspan, and everyone cheers.

The sun peeks out of the water at the horizon. Everyone who's not jumping stands in front of them, phones out, filming it. One, two, three, and they all jump. Still in slow motion, I watch everyone fall to the ground, land hard, begin to shout in pain. One person grabs the side of the railing and hangs there, screaming, then finally drops. The watchers are cheering at first, then their faces turn to shock when the group hits the ground. A guy who was below Jess tries to catch her, and she crashes on top of him.

I take a sip of my coffee. What is going on?

CHAPTER 37:

The fog is thick. Carol joins me at the dock, and I'm unsurprised to see her.

"Carol, do you notice the in-between spaces?"

She looks at me, expression confused. "I'm not sure I know what you mean, Emily."

"Do you notice what's in between? You know, what's not said, the pauses in between what people say, silences? When things are quiet, the truth is there."

"Emily, are you all right? You seem a little off today. I don't think I get what you're asking."

"People say many things, and they lie to themselves and to other people about what's really going on."

Carol shrugs. "I mean, maybe there was a time when I wouldn't always speak the truth, but that comes as you get older."

"That's not what I mean. Tell me what's going on with the Howards. What happened to them? I know you know what happened to them. I'm tired of you pretending that everything is mysterious when even I know that you'd have found out what happened. You'd never let a story like that go."

Just asking the question drained me. But it needed to be said, was there already and just needed a push.

"They're fine. They live in North Carolina. Karen reconnected with her daughter. She's in nursing school now. One of the kids is a senior in high school, and the other is in their second year of college at a university. Fred found a great job, and the family is thriving."

"So they never went insane?"

"I didn't say that."

I can't see much more than five feet in front of me because the fog is so dense, but I catch glimpses of movement and notice a boat coming up slowly. Two anglers are inside, heads tilted down, poles in the water. The boat moves slowly along the shore. Almost like they're in a separate world, they pass the dock in silence. One of them tilts his head in recognition.

CHAPTER 38:

"Em-i-ly" I wake up to someone whispering. "Em-i-ly" I get out of bed to investigate. I look from the top of the basement stairs and see Mei disappear into the basement. I follow her down.

When I open the basement door and walk inside, it's not the basement, but Mei's house thirteen years ago. I'd only ever been in Mei's house that one day—the day it all happened. But this is exactly how I remember it. The red couch in the living room, the smell of a home-cooked meal lingering in the background. Shoes organized at the foyer.

Mei hums in the kitchen. I can tell she's content. Michael runs to her, and she picks him up and mumbles something in Chinese. She hugs him, and he takes off to play with his cars in the living room. A waft of authentic Chinese food hits my nostrils. I go to the kitchen and watch her cook; she doesn't miss a beat. Her movements are fluid. There's something about seeing Mei chop vegetables and mother her son that makes me smile inside. I don't want to disturb her. I want to watch her like this forever and erase the other memories that I have of her. I want this to be her story. I wonder if this happened back then. I think it did.

I know I can talk to Mei, but I'm afraid to disrupt her happiness. I'm the one who brings sadness to them; it's not fair that I do that.

As Mei turns on the rice cooker, she looks at me. "I let go of the past. You bring it back."

Her face turns serious again, and I'm worried she'll get upset. I try to deflect.

"I'm happy to see you with Michael."

Mei turns back to cooking as if she doesn't hear me. She finishes what she's doing, then walks past me. I feel the need to follow her, so I do.

She opens a door to what looks like their garage and leaves it open. I follow her inside, but it's not her garage. It's my house, thirteen years ago. Recognition hits, and I bury my face in my hands. The room spins, and the emotions come on with no invitation. I don't want to see what happens next; it'll be too much for me to handle. I remove my hands from my eyes, and Mei is in front of me, staring. "Your house, long time ago. You need to see it."

I walk around the corner from the foyer to the living room, and no one is there. I keep walking and see Sienna at the age of three sitting at the dining table. I'm there too, reading her a book. She's listening, and I'm animating the words. She smiles and listens, hanging on to what I'm saying. She asks questions, and her three-year-old voice makes a piece of me melt. The yearning to have that time back is overwhelming. What I want more than ever is to capture how I might have been feeling at that time and feel it now. I have an intense desire to cherish and enjoy every second of the time she sits next to me while we read the book.

I drop to my knees. Mei comes to me. "You cry and cry. Why you cry when you have beautiful child?"

I'm confused as to why Mei has everything together, until I realize she's not dealing with the truth of the situation. "Mei, I can't change what happened."

"Emily, I can't change what happened. Why do you make pain for yourself in your heart? Love your family instead of cry."

"I was scared of what happened to you. I was afraid it would happen to me. I was afraid to be a mom. I was also depressed. Like you."

Mei shook her head sadly. "I can't change what happened, but I know you need change. You hurt so much; you miss your life. You waste the good, what matters. You suffer because you give up on self. You think you don't matter."

"It's not that simple."

CHAPTER 39:

The sun warms my belly. The temperature is spot-on for a swimsuit on the dock but not a dip in the water—not just yet. Sun hits my face, and an array of clouds spread out. Distant chatter in the background, words unintelligible. The scene is relaxing and calm, a safe place to be. A boat motors past. Gentle waves roll in, and the dock sways. I'm fully in this moment, but not quite. What's poking my side? It's like a bug flying around me. An unsettling feeling lingers. My finger can't place it. Frustration at not being able to enjoy the moment, dammit. Why?

And then it strikes me, like a ball hitting my head from behind—no warning, just a shot through the heart. My mind travels back.

A tragic story starts with laughter and lightness and ends with doom and gloom, but this story doesn't roll like that. It beats to a different drum. This is how my story went.

Sienna was two, almost three, full of energy and curiosity. My job was to maintain the household and care for Sienna. Every morning the same: get up with Sienna, breakfast, then parents' morning out, lunch, then keep Sienna occupied, clean up, cook dinner, Kyle comes home, clean up, then fight to get Sienna to go to bed.

Our neighborhood thrived, filled with educated young parents who hung out, laughed, and had block parties every week. It was as if I was looking in from the outside at happiness that everyone could feel but I was not privy to. They didn't exclude me; I don't blame them. All it would have taken was one other mom. A person to connect and gossip with, have drinks with on Fridays, sit with to watch the kids run around in the yard. But it was as if they could sense me repelling them. Depression doesn't attract people.

I was that person before Sienna, the one who included everyone. People wanted to be around me, but that changed after she was born. Attraction died out, and I didn't want it back.

I encouraged isolation, and isolated I was. I couldn't draw or paint either. The most I managed were sketches at night before I fell asleep. Showing Kyle a sketch or two, receiving a grunt or a head nod, and then back to the next episode he was watching. Life should have been nice and fulfilling, but it felt empty and wrong.

The best part of my day was drinking coffee after dropping Sienna off at parents' morning out, sitting at the kitchen table and looking out my living room window. It was the best view in the neighborhood. I spent pointless hours there when I could have been painting, sketching, or doing something for myself. People walking their dogs, retirees going for their daily stroll, moms pushing strollers, kids riding bikes around the block, and the occasional deer. And then there was…Mei.

Kyle had told me about them. Mei was a stay-at-home mom from China who had recently moved into the neighborhood with her husband, who had gotten a research job at Emory University. Mei had Michael, who was about the same age as Sienna, and a young baby boy. She walked around the neighborhood at the same time every day, chasing Michael around. Screaming at him to slow down, watch for cars, don't go too far. Sometimes he would stay in the stroller, and other times he ran free. He was an active two-year-old, a bit out of control. Seeing Mei made me feel like a normal mom, even if just for those short moments.

I wondered if she felt like me and if we could connect. I thought I should go out there and talk to her, become friends with her. We both needed help with our toddlers. Who didn't need a friend? But I didn't do it. I didn't once introduce myself as a neighbor.

One time, Michael ran to my door and knocked, much to his mother's dismay. When I went to the door and said "Hello," he ran back to his mom. Mei waved and laughed and said, "Sorry."

That was my chance to say something. Ask her to meet up for a playdate. But I just stood there. I waved and said, "It's okay." That was it. I didn't do anything else; a missed opportunity I will forever regret.

I don't want to recall the next time I saw Mei; it's too much for anyone to take. A few weeks after my missed opportunity to be friends with Mei, our lives collided, and nothing was ever the same.

According to my watch, Mei and her boys were ten minutes later than usual that day. It was at that point I saw a woman walking alone, and it took me a few seconds to realize it was Mei. No stroller, and no Michael. She walked as if she'd just run a marathon, out of breath and dazed, in her own world. Something struck me as odd. That thought was even more validated when Mei turned the corner into our cul-de-sac. She had blood all over the front of her shirt.

My instincts kicked in, and I ran out the door. Mei was mumbling to herself in Mandarin. She stopped in front of me but looked through me, not at me, still mumbling.

I asked, "Mei, are you all right? You have blood on your shirt."

Her eyes darted, her demeanor off. The day took on an oppressive quality, as if a tornado was about to pass through. Or maybe I just remember it that way. Mei looked down and began to scream, piercing shrieks coming from her throat.

"Mei, are you hurt?"

Mei cried, "I think my son dead."

"What! Where is he?" I yelled.

"Help, please help." She covered her face with her hands and shook her head.

"Where is he?"

Not saying anything, she turned and ran back toward her house. I followed her. My gut was in my throat, and acidity rose, burning. I was running as fast as I could, yet it felt like it took me ten times longer to get to her house than it should have. My heart was beating fast, and my mind was racing, the sense that something was desperately wrong surrounding me. It was nauseating.

What I found in that house was something I never thought I'd ever encounter. Samuel, her three-month-old baby, was crying, alone in a swing. I saw a bloody knife on the floor. Uneasiness crept up my spine.

I followed Mei to the upstairs bedroom to find sheets filled with pools of blood covering a small body. I looked at Mei in disbelief, tears forming as I began to catch on to what had happened. I looked at her with weepy eyes. "What happened?"

I still can't believe she said it. "I think I killed my son." She dropped to her knees and wailed, covering her head.

Much as I didn't want to see, I had to pull the covers back. His throat was cut from one side to the other, a clean cut.

Michael was already gone, and I cried not for him, but for Mei. She finally raised her head, and when I met her eyes, I saw something distant and sick, something besides herself, something dark. Something familiar.

I'd seen her pull Michael from the street, away from a UPS truck flying around the corner. I'd seen her call out in distress when she couldn't see him when he'd wandered too close to the woods. I'd thought she was overprotective.

It's the space between the breaths, the moments we miss in life and don't see. How could a mother do this to her own child? It's counterintuitive, unfathomable; you can't imagine it. And yet, before you can even be angry, grief takes over like a bulldozer and flattens your heart before it can beat again.

Her tragedy is now my tragedy. We are connected. Instead of befriending her and perhaps reading these signs or cushioning the effects of depression, I met her at her most vulnerable time in life, and I saw her destiny flash in front of my eyes. How does this story end well? How do you ever recover from this?

The police were called, the father came, and Mei was taken off in handcuffs. One would think, in a situation like this, that you would want the mother to pay for her actions. She needed to have her day of reckoning for what she'd done. However, I saw this mother's weakness, so raw and submissive, as she realized what she'd done. Like dates written in a history book, this date was etched in my mind.

Later, Kyle spoke to Mei's husband to give our condolences. All Mei's husband could say in disbelief was, "My wife is loving. She loves her children; she loved Michael. She is loving."

It affected everyone in the neighborhood. Some got closer, and others became more isolated. No one wanted to talk to me. What do you say to the mother who witnessed the aftermath of the crime scene? Nothing. Like they had to fend off germs, neighbors masked themselves from me.

What irked me the most was that I was Mei. I could have been in her shoes. She went to prison, and it could have been me. So I became Mei, a Mei who was free. Tortured by the illness, I was determined to represent the life Mei could have led as a free woman. Mirroring the misfortune, damning myself to suffer for her sins.

I asked myself over and over, is prison appropriate for a mother who slays her child? Are we protecting the world from her? Or are we protecting her from us? Protecting ourselves from the truth that any one of us could be Mei. Some people judged Mei and wished death on her. That would have been a gift to Mei. What was hardest to comprehend was how Mei went from a loving mother to murdering her own child. Did people think about her mental state before they passed judgment? The judgment of... Those actions have nothing to do with me. But don't they? Do they not? Are you a human with great powers who can create and destroy? How do you know that could never be you?

Those people didn't have the perspective I had, looking Mei in the face as she came back to reality from a moment of insanity. I saw her. I saw the transformation happen in front of my eyes.

Push it away. Don't talk about it. Mental illness. What a downer. Judgment. What a freak. How do you bring it up in casual conversations without being inappropriate? You don't; it's inappropriate. It's not there; you should be happy. Although it happened right under our noses, in front of us, we don't want to see it.

Mei was culturally isolated, no village to support her. She had a husband who loved her but didn't know how bad her depression had become or where her breaking point was. Police reports said Mei's husband had been getting concerned about her mental state and temper before it occurred. When is too much? How can you possibly know? Why didn't I befriend her?

Every day the same—same routine, keep the routine, it's better for the kids. Until, snap, the routine goes to shit.

But isn't it easy to be a mom? All you have to do is take care of the kids—it's easy. They can't stop crying; you can't stop crying. No sleep tonight, no sleep tomorrow night. Haven't been able to shower in three days. Feeding, breast-feeding. It confers the mother's antibodies. It's the healthy way. Don't stop. Nipples bleeding, keep feeding, keep feeding, the baby's mouth rips the scab off. It's the healthy way, the mother's way. Go alone into a room, away from people, and feed your baby. The baby is crying. Stop your sleep, your conversation, and feed that baby. You're the mother. Cover yourself in public. Who do you think you are? Your baby is crying. Why is she crying? You're the mother, you should know. Fix it; the crying bothers me.

Don't say no to your child; always say yes. Don't let them smell your fear; show them who's boss. Protect them, protect them, protect them. Don't let them out of your sight. Don't hit them; do hit them. No electronics, but sometimes electronics. Don't shout at them; reason with them. Don't let them eat this; do let them eat that. Shut your child up, it's disruptive in public. Geez, kids these days, no one parents them anymore. No relief. It's your turn to take care of the child. You're the mom. I did it last night. I worked all day, what did you do? And why is the house such a mess?

My child was much better off in my womb; now she is out, and I don't know what to do. Who knows what to do?

Generational changes, the information age, technology growth, globalization. How can we expect that something isn't going to falter? No one told me this would happen, but it wouldn't have mattered had I known—the engine is more powerful than its parts.

I had a choice. I could fight the pressure from myself, from Kyle, and from my culture, but I didn't. I had no idea it was occurring. The only tool I had was to run—run away from motherhood. Protect your child because you're not worthy of her existence; worse, you could harm her. My choice, the unnatural decision to turn my back on instincts, tainted by an experience that marked me for life. Suppressing your liberation comes with a cost—a cost that might end badly. I no longer trusted myself. I could no longer suppress the longing to be free from motherhood.

So I ran. The night Michael died, a piece of me died too. He wasn't my child, but I did it for Mei. I owed it to her. I could have befriended Mei, but I didn't. I'll forever regret not being there or seeing what could have been avoided if only I'd invited her into my home and had her son play with Sienna. I've rewritten the moment Michael walked up to my door, but it never changed anything. That was the same night I left Kyle in my mind. Nine months later, our divorce was final. Sienna was three, and she didn't see me again for a year and three months. I disappeared from that life and created a new one. I became… the mother on the side.

My consciousness comes back to where I am now, the dock rocking to the waves, the air warm on my belly, and the sun in my face. The story is done. That's what happened. I was hungry before, but now I'm not. The nauseating feeling of darkness has stifled my appetite.

I stand up and swallow the lump in my throat. It travels down to my gut and festers for a moment. It remains there—a seed of truth. Maybe some good ramen broth will be the antidote to the darkness, chicken soup for the soul in hopes of covering this seed of shame.

CHAPTER 40:

I wake up in bed again, pain going down my neck. I feel like I didn't sleep yet. My brain is on overdrive. I don't know how many days it's been since I left the cabin, but I have no desire to do anything else but be here. I want to keep seeing Mei and Michael. I'm getting used to seeing them, and I want to know what's happening. I'm scared of them for what they might be, and I don't know what to expect from either of them, but there's an understanding that has formed between us that I count on.

I go down to the basement on my own and search for Mei and Michael. I look around but can't find them. I sit on the floor in the basement and smell the dirty, musty odor. It used to be creepy, the rancid smell of death, the dark corners, the faint streaks of light that hit retired cobwebs. However, there's something familiar about this scene that I have an intense desire to experience.

My thoughts wander. The fear of change, the loss of direction, not knowing the right thing to do. The amount of passion that leaves you when something so pure leaves your life. I can't go back and redo it. I sit there in this nastiness. I want to feel it all over me. I take off my clothes, feel the coldness of the concrete floor. Particles of dirt attach to my body. I roll around, create imaginary snow angels. I feel a mess of cobwebs in my hair. I lie back, and the light coming through the old, cracked windows illuminates the dust circulating in the air. I feel a sense of reprieve, and I allow this experience to take me over. I'm cold and uncomfortable, but somehow the discomfort is comforting. Perhaps this is the naked portrait the ghost will paint of me, naked on the floor covered in cobwebs, dust, and pieces of dead bugs.

I fall asleep, and when I wake up, it's pitch black. I manage to find my clothes by feel and put them back on. There's no light, nothing reflecting off the water or from a bright star. I feel my way around, feel everything I touch carefully, try to make sense of my surroundings. There's dirt on my feet, which doesn't protect me from the hard metal nails. I step on a tack, and my foot bleeds. I find a doorknob. I turn it, but it doesn't open; locked. I finally locate the door to the stairs that lead to the main part of the house, but when I try the doorknob, it's locked too.

At first, I'm fine with it. I'm okay that I can't get out. I want to see Mei and Michael. But the wait is long. The passing of time seems like days, but no daylight finds its way into the basement. Time ticks by, and nothing. Mei and Michael never show up. If they were here, I could at least fill my time with watching them happy together. I could spend hours, days, years, watching them together again.

The light never shows, and the door never unlocks. I'm stuck here. I walk the perimeter of the basement. There has to be a way out. I only find two doors: one to the outside, and one into the main part of the house. They're locked. I don't know what to do with myself, and finally the fact that I'm trapped starts getting to me.

I kick the door to the main house and scream for someone to let me out. I stumble around the basement mumbling to myself. I'm confused and disoriented. I scream for Mei and Michael, but they never answer me. Then I get mad at them for not being here for me when I'm in such a vulnerable place. I wonder if they're the ones keeping me down here—if they locked me out of the main part of the house. I feel betrayed because Mei seemed like she was trying to help me, and now she has disappeared. I punch at one of the windows, but it doesn't break. The sun never comes. I'll die down here.

After a long time, I sit back down on the floor. I'm not well, and my mind is fried. I think about Sienna, but I don't cry. She wanted someone else, someone strong and present. I lost her before I could even be an influence in her life.

As I'm thinking about the reality of my situation, I see a light in the darkness. I stand up and walk toward it. And there, in the corner, is Sienna at the age of sixteen. I want to reach out to her, but the real Sienna wouldn't let me touch her. She'd brush me to the side, disappointed in me. She sits there looking at me. There are so many things I want to say, but no words come out. *I'm sorry* seems like the wrong thing to say in this situation. *I could have done better, and I will* sounds like a weak promise.

I settle with, "I'm so happy to see you."

Sienna looks at me. "You know, Mom, things aren't that bad now."

"What do you mean?"

"I play soccer all the time. People are nice to me. You know, I didn't like many people before. They annoyed me. But now things are better."

"I'm glad things have changed for you."

"It's like they understand me."

"I'd imagine everyone is more accepting."

"Yes, I feel better. I can sleep."

"That's so great, honey."

I blink, and she's gone. I look around for her, but I know her presence has left. A sense of relief fills me, knowing that she's okay, but the coldness and vulnerability return quickly. I hear something coming from upstairs, and a sense of excitement runs through me.

I walk to the door and put my ear to it. There are people talking in the main area of the cabin. It sounds like two women. Carol's voice, and maybe Chastain's? I can't make out what they're saying, but I hear my name. Their words are blunted by the door and the distance. I feel like this is my chance to get out, so I bang on the door. I stop and listen, but no one comes. I do it over and over again, and they still don't come.

I think they left, but no, I can still hear them talking. I scream as loud as I can, like my life depends on it. I stop and listen.

It *is* Chastain's voice. "Did you hear that?"

Carol responds, "No, but my hearing isn't what it used to be."

I get a thrill. I scream out Chastain's name, then stop and listen.

Chastain says, "I must be hearing things."

Carol says, "Maybe it's kids screaming outside."

I hear footsteps heading toward the porch, and I scream again. "No, Chastain, I'm down here! Down in the basement. I'm here. I'm here!"

Tears roll down my face, and I turn with my back pressed against the door and slide down to the floor. I cry into my bent knees. I don't hear anyone above anymore. Helplessness penetrates me, and weakness takes over. I'm stuck.

I want to bang my head on the door until the frustration causes physical pain. I want to give up. But as soon as that thought enters my mind, something else joins it. Giving up isn't an option. Possibility is the drumbeat that pushes my legs to step one foot in front of the other. I trip over and over again, and I'm on the floor for long periods of time, but staying on the floor and disappearing into the earth is not an option for me.

No brilliant ideas come to my mind. Darkness is everywhere, and it clouds my mind, sight, and hearing, covers my skin, invades the depths of my body. But the darkness ends at my soul. It provides light, even though I can't see it inside myself. It guides me places. It guided me here.

I rack my brain to figure out what I can do to get out, but I've exhausted all the possibilities. Acceptance is my only choice. I'm here. I'm trapped, and I can't do anything about it. I'm sad. I want to do other things. I miss being around friends. I have a sense of appreciation for people that I've never felt before. My mind runs through the things I love about the people in my life. I hear Chas's laugh echo through the empty basement. I see Arin's eyebrows move up, feel her energy. I crave the people who surround me in this town. I want to live more than I ever have before. To have the touch of another, experience the conflict that they bring, the difficulties, the stress and irritation, along with the good stuff.

I find what feels like a broom by the washer and dryer, and I start sweeping. A pile of dirt is gathering, and my feet feel for it. I sweep and sweep. I organize the clutter and organize the space as best I can. Lifejackets piled with lifejackets. Oars leaning in a corner. Rafts, some with air still left in them, emptied and folded on top of one another. I find an empty jar to hold the nails and tacks that I keep stepping on, that wound the bottom of my feet. I place the scattered tools inside an old toolbox. An old rag clears out the cobwebs from the windowsills. I find a container and place the swept-up dust and dirt in it. I feel better, like I have a purpose. If I can't do what I want to do, then I'll find purpose in something else.

But the room I'm in is changing. Things I couldn't see before are becoming clearer. I see outlines. Depth perception is getting keener. My sense of smell grows stronger. Slight puffs of air give me information I wouldn't have picked up on before. My senses finally open.

What I feared when I first got to the cabin is no longer something to fear. It's something to accept. It's my world here. The objects around me keep me occupied. I don't want to be here, but I choose to believe that one day I'll get out of this.

Push-ups and planks, coming up with new ways to keep my body active, something I do twice a day. I make sure my heart rate speeds up and slows. I don't eat anything but drink water from the sink. I'm not hungry, only thirsty. I don't know how long my days will continue like this. There is no deadline. At times, the belief that I will never get out invades my mind. I cry out in anger at myself for being here. Until…

CHAPTER 41:

I wake up and find I can't move. I'm paralyzed in my space. God isn't really God; He is the devil. I question His power. I was able to make the best of my situation, being in the dark, locked basement, and now I can't even move. Wait. Yes I can. I can move my fingers and toes, bend my knees about three-fourths of the way, raise my arms about an inch, and move my head from side to side. Claustrophobia kicks in, and my heart rate increases until I'm in a full-blown panic attack. I yearn for the freedom to roam the basement, the ability to sweep, feel the coldness of my vulnerability, not be tied to this small space. I finally manage to calm my anxiety, and I laugh out loud at the absurdity. I yearn to exercise my body. Sweat beads on my skin.

I still see nothing; has it gotten darker? I wonder if I'm in a box. There's something surrounding me, and it feels stringy and stretchy.

I don't want to go to sleep. I'm afraid I won't wake up again. I become obsessed with freedom and fantasize about being somewhere else. My imagination takes over. I feel people close to me. I can almost smell them, feel their energy around me. I want it to be true. Am I making it up in my head? Yet again, I'm faced with the thought, can I just die?

I won't give up. I *will* make it to freedom. I allow my imagination to run free. I create stories and conflicts, and my mind is full of another world.

I can see. I was wondering if my eyes had stopped functioning and I'd lost my eyesight, but no. I've been envisioning that I'm buried alive.

The light gets brighter and brighter, and I see I'm trapped in white, sticky, stringy material. The more I stretch, the more I find space to move. I keep wiggling.

I poke my finger, and it seems to penetrate a layer of the material. After poking through many layers, I feel air. I'm able to spread and stretch the tiny hole that I created with my finger and get my hand, wrist, arm, then my shoulder out. Little by little, my body comes out of this weblike stuff. I find myself falling to the floor, and the sunlight hits my face. I haven't seen light in so long that every time I open my lids, my eyes water. I cover them with my hands and turn to face an area that isn't as bright. I open my eyes a little, then quickly close them. Again and again, I try to open them, making it longer each time.

I can see ahead of me. I haven't ever witnessed a brighter day in my life. I look around, and I'm still in the basement. I look out the windows to the lake. The light seems surreal, likely because of the amount of time I spent in the dark.

I move to the door because I know I'm free at this point. I could walk through walls right now, no problem. I open the door to the outside. The sun is shining, and the world seems bigger. The sparkle of the lake water reflecting the sun seems more radiant than ever before. That's when I notice them. They're lined up in a row holding hands. Mei, Michael, and Sienna are looking at the water, standing there at the edge. They all turn around and wave at me. I wave back. They turn back toward the water. Their bodies smudge out like paint smearing, and the shadows that were their bodies turn to tiny particles that sparkle. The sparkles, like magic, become part of the reflection off the water.

I'm drawn to it and walk to the water, walk in, following the sparkles. I feel the warmth of the water. It gets higher and higher until it's over my head. I sink into the depths of the lake. I'm falling to the bottom.

CHAPTER 42:

I wake up in a hospital room. I'm connected to wires, oxygen, an IV, and I hear beeping from machines. No one is in the room, and it's daylight out. I see a table with a bunch of flowers on it.

A nurse walks into the room. She smiles at me. "Glad to see you're awake."

"What happened?"

"Your friends pulled you out of Lake Lure. You're lucky to be alive. You were unconscious, severely dehydrated, and malnourished."

"What friends pulled me out?"

"A woman named Chastain and another, Carol. They've been visiting you since you got here."

"How long have I been unconscious?"

"A few days. How are you feeling?"

"I don't know, really. Strange."

"It's normal to feel disoriented after something like this. Do you have any pain?"

I take stock of my body. "I don't think so."

"Well, okay. I'm going to get the doctor."

She leaves, and the doctor comes in a few minutes later. He asks me a bunch of questions. As the day moves on, I feel better.

I look at my body. Have I lost weight? I reflect on being at the cabin and what happened in the basement. Or was it a bad dream?

I reach for a remote on the side of the bed and turn on the TV. I flip through channels, not really paying attention to anything on the screen. I can't focus. I feel disconnected from what's been going on in the world. I had been in my microcosm dealing with my own stuff for only about a month, but it was really thirteen years.

Like a snap, a blink, a stomp, the burden I've carried lifts, flutters away from me. A seed that was carried away to somewhere else. The lightness of this realization makes me want to do something big, make grand changes in my life. My perspective has changed. It's not the same life I had a month ago. The dullness has now brightened. I think about hope instead of doom. Mostly, I think about Sienna and how important it is to have her in my life, how much I miss her. I know I want her back in my life.

I try to focus on the news. My being has been reset, calibrated to the understanding of the workings of humanity, my own humanity. I listen to a report from Atlanta—*Mother released after serving thirteen years in prison for murdering her son due to postpartum psychosis.*

I see Mei leaving jail after serving her sentence. Her husband embraces her as Mei exits to her freedom. One tear trickles down my face. My emotions fray. I think about what I would say to Mei, but no. I'd only hug her. There's nothing I could say to her that would match what I feel inside.

I drift in and out of sleep. I wake up at one point, and both Carol and Chastain are in the room with me. Chastain walks over to my bedside with a wet face.

She smiles through her tears. "Can we stop this shit? Where are we? Are we okay?"

I figure I deserve this, under the circumstances. I don't know what happened, but as far as I can put together, she fished me out of the lake.

"I'm fine. Really, I am. Thank you, Chas."

"Okay. We're alive, and we're fine. Life is worth living, and we're going to participate in it, like a hundred percent, right?"

"Yes, Chas, we're in it a hundred percent."

"Okay, now you owe me. If I'm ever drowning, you've got my back, right?"

"Yes, of course I'll be there."

Chastain's phone rings. She answers it, and then she hands the phone to me. "It's Arin. You know her ass is all the way in Japan right now."

"Hey, Arin."

"Oh my gosh, babe, how are you doing?"

"I'm okay. Good—better now."

"I'm so happy to hear your voice. What happened? Did you drink too much and sleepwalk into the lake?"

"That's a good question. I don't know how I got there. Chas, how did I end up in the water?"

Chas looks at me, half in disbelief and half in annoyance. "I drove up after you hadn't answered my phone calls and texts for days. I went to Carol's house, and we searched for you all over the house."

"Did you go into the basement?"

"Of course we went into the basement, but we didn't see you."

I'm struck by this. I'd been stuck in that basement. I knew every square inch of it. I stay quiet and let her continue. "Then Carol and I went to the police station, and we were on our way back from filing a missing person report when there you were, walking like a zombie to the water. And then you just sank into the lake."

Her expression changes to fear and sadness as she continues. "You didn't come back up, so I ran out to the water. At first I couldn't see you, but then I saw something shimmering in the water, so I went toward it, and it was you. I pulled you up, and you weren't responsive. You coughed out a bunch of water, and you were breathing but not conscious."

I exhale heavily. "I'm sorry, Chas."

I don't want to describe why I went into the water or my experience in the basement. Too much unpacking to do.

Arin says, "That's so scary, Em. Glad you're okay. Thank goodness for Chas being there at the right time."

"Thank you for calling me, Arin. How is Japan?"

"Oh, Em, stop it. Japan is Japan. We can talk about that at the exhibit. Chas told me you were busy and have several pieces of artwork that look amazing."

I chat with Arin for a few minutes, and then we hang up.

Chas says, "Sorry I didn't bring you flowers. I was too busy saving your ass."

An uncontrollable laugh bellows out of me like it has been caged. The doctor comes in right then and lets me know I'm well enough to be discharged, and Chas and I go back to the cabin.

CHAPTER 43:

Chas and I grab bottles of sparkling water and head for the dock. She asks me about the cabin and if I think it's haunted. The best answer I can give her is that it brings out the ghosts and the traumas that you carry and forces you to look at them. I tell her I believe that it's not a haunting, but more of an opportunity to heal. I explain how my arm seemed to have a mind of its own, and it resulted in the paintings I finished, and how some sort of force kept me going. Chas shrugs and shakes her head. She doesn't understand, but I think she believes me.

Then she gets serious. "Em, why were you walking into the water like that? Should I be worried?"

I explain that I was chasing the traumas of my past into the water. They're gone now, and I can rest. I've worked things out.

She stares at me as if trying to decide whether she believes me or not. Or maybe she thinks I'm nuts. In the end, she says, "I'm happy to hear that, Em."

Chastain's phone rings. She says a few words to the caller and then hands me the phone. "I guess I'm your answering service now." She gives me a hard look. "It's Kyle."

My heart skips a beat. Chas tells me she's going back inside as I take the phone. "Hey, Kyle."

"Hey, Em. Are you okay?"

"Yes, I'm fine, thanks to Chas."

"Are you really okay? Because it didn't sound like you were okay."

"Yes. It's a long story, but I'm better than I was before. Much better. I promise."

"So, Em, the other reason I called is because I want to apologize for things that have happened in the past, explain some things."

I can't imagine there's anything he needs to apologize to me for. He's been an amazing dad. "There's nothing you need to apologize for. I wasn't there the way I should have been. I just couldn't get it right, Kyle."

"Listen, Em, I know what happened to Mei and Michael really hit you hard. It would have anyone. I wasn't there for you the way you needed me to be, and I'm sorry."

"I don't blame you for it, and I don't know what you could have done to resolve it."

"There's more I want to say. When Sienna got kidnapped..."

"What about it?"

"You went to the wrong location; instead of going to the academy, you went to the school."

"Right, I went to the school first."

"Laura told you it was at the school; you didn't get it wrong."

"What do you mean?"

"I'm trying to tell you that Laura intentionally lied to you about where Sienna was, and she's done it several times before. At first I thought it was an accident, but then I started catching on that she never forgets these things and is amazing at scheduling and location stuff. I knew she'd given you the wrong information when we were at the police station, but it would have caused too much drama and taken focus away from Sienna if I'd confronted her. I kept it in as long as I could, until I finally exploded at her."

"Why would she do something like that? I didn't need help ruining my relationship with Sienna."

The information doesn't sit well in my stomach. What type of person sabotages someone else like that? Something so sacred as a parent-child bond. How could she let jealousy and callousness get in the way of such an important relationship as that between a mother and daughter?

"I don't know why. Maybe she felt threatened by you. She found your weakness and preyed on it."

The anger boils inside me. "She was intentionally sabotaging our relationship? That's beyond fucked up, Kyle."

"I didn't know what else to do but tell you the truth. I'm enraged by what she did."

"How do we go back and correct this? Why isn't Laura apologizing to me or explaining herself?"

"After I exploded, we split up. We're getting a divorce. There were other issues that I've overlooked through the years. I didn't want to split up another marriage, was worried what it would do to Sienna."

I've spent so much time thinking that everything was my fault. The guilt I suffered. The time I wasted thinking that I was the worst human being on the planet for not picking her up before someone kidnapped her. I think about what kind of person would do this. And then it dawns on me.

"Did Laura have something to do with the kidnapping?"

"I don't think she would ever be mixed up with something like that, but I went to the police and told them what happened. Let's just say she filed for divorce the next day. The police called her in for questioning, and they haven't found any evidence that links her to the kidnappers, if that gives you any peace of mind. Plus, she had no idea you'd forget your phone. She did admit it went too far. Laura liked being the one Sienna went to and didn't want you to get in the way. She was jealous of you and didn't want you near Sienna or me."

"Why didn't you tell me?"

"I didn't piece all of it together until then. I was shocked, and it all came to a head at once... I'm sorry, Em. I can't say that enough. I'm sorry for everything."

I exhale thirteen years of confusion and sadness out of my system.

"Thanks for telling me, Kyle. I'm sorry for everything that's happened and my part in it. I need to let you go now."

I hang up the phone. And sit there.

The relief is like a punch to my gut. It knocks the wind out of me. If I hadn't been so depressed all those years, I might have caught on to what Laura was doing. I'd viewed everything as my fault but didn't stop to consider that other people could damage things too. I took too much responsibility for things I couldn't control and then was oblivious to Laura's nastiness. I'm heartbroken all over again, but in a different way.

Chastain walks back over and sits next to me. "So now it's my turn to explain some things."

I turn to her. "What do you mean?"

"I know what happened with Laura. Kyle told me. We all know. Arin, Carol, everyone knows. You didn't think we would get involved?"

"What do you mean? Why wouldn't you tell me?"

"You refused to open up to the therapist, and you were still in so much distress over leaving and what happened with Mei. Kyle didn't want to tell you until you made some progress. He was worried it was too much for you to handle. When Arin told us about this strange, haunted, magical cabin, we were desperate. You know Arin and all her crazy beliefs. But we had to do something. It sounds like Arin was right. I'm not the one who's going to tell her that, though. Her ego is already way too big."

I smile and look out at the lake.

Chastain continues. "You were treading water for way too long. If Arin had said we should snap our fingers three times, hop on one foot, etc., we would have tried it."

"You knowingly sent me to a haunted cabin to wash away my troubles? I don't know what to say."

"Look at the bright side; you came here, met some interesting people, got all your artwork ready for the exhibit, and almost died. Well, that wasn't part of the fucking plan. Jesus, I'm glad I got here when I did."

"How would you respond to what Laura did?"

"She was a suspect in Sienna's kidnapping, and they questioned her. You know if I smell anything foul, I'll be knocking on the detective's door with some cold, hard evidence."

"How do you know all these people here?"

"Oh, Carol knows Arin through some art collector friends. That's how we found out about the history of the cabin."

"Oh yeah, Mariam and George. Do you know who owns the cabin?"

"No. That I don't know."

I sit there thinking. I'm frustrated by the amount of effort that went into this whole charade. I stare out onto the lake and its beauty. The dependable mountains still stage the backdrop. The lake sparkles in the setting sun, and the trees are vibrant. I feel this moment in its entirety. I'm not hiding what happened in the past. I know so much more now. There's a hardness to the truth about the part the main character in my story played. The biggest thing I learned is that it makes no sense to hate myself. We all make mistakes. My intentions were in the right place, but fear threw me off my path.

I don't fear life, making mistakes, or the darkness. Darkness is never forgiving yourself, making the same mistakes over and over again, staying the same without the willingness to change the harm you do to yourself and others. I'm just as bad as Laura, because I gave up. I let her come in and take over. It's interesting how darkness enters while you're weak and vulnerable.

I stand up with dignity and strength like the mountain. I'm resilient like the trees bordering the shore, and I cleanse myself of my past with the lake's water and move forward. I turn and look at Chastain.

"You know what, Chas? I've got things to do."
She smiles and says, "That's my girl."

CHAPTER 44:

Arin's gallery is a renovated historical home in the city of Atlanta. She's spent more time preparing for the Metamorphosis exhibit than for any other. She wants it to be the highlight of my career.

Fresh red rose petals cover the black-and-white flooring. The entire space smells like a rose garden. There's one room where artists are making shapes with the rose petals during the exhibit. A group of violinists play in a corner. The walls are painted black. The attire is dressy, but attendees were instructed in the invitations to leave their shoes at the entrance and feel the rose petals on their feet. Waiters with black-and-white tuxedos and butterfly bow ties serve foods that represent transformation: salad cups with iceberg lettuce cut into shapes of butterflies filled with a mixture of veggies and topped with an herbed lemon vinaigrette, vegan frog leg–shaped portabella mushrooms, and edible flowers. Red wine spills lavishly out of a fountain to whimsically splash into glasses. Three overweight black cats with pearl collars roam the gallery, rub against legs, and laze on the floor. Large crystal chandeliers light each room of the gallery.

My artwork includes paintings, sketches, and prints. The featured painting depicts a realistic beating heart, but the heart resembles the body of a butterfly, wings sticking out and blood dripping from the sides. Another painting is of a woman walking naked through a crowd of clothed people on the street, chains around her hands and feet. Some of the people are looking at her, and others aren't, but she looks straight ahead. I've painted a portrait of a White woman looking in a mirror, but in her refection is a woman of a different ethnicity. I look at the one I've done in a childlike style, similar to the one I painted of the boxed black butterfly, only this painting is of a butterfly flying free from a black box.

I'm the calmest I've ever been at an exhibit. All the pieces speak to me on a deep level. My artwork represents a time that I want to relegate to my past. Selling these pieces is yet another step in leaving my past behind and moving forward.

My paintings line the walls in three rooms of the gallery. As I walk around, everyone congratulates me and says how brilliant everything looks. I'm comfortable in my skin, but it seems like something is missing. After I make contact with every person there, I make my way to the rose petal design room where two kids are doing snow angels and another two pile them up to jump in. There's satisfaction in seeing them blissfully carry on for the mere purpose of enjoyment. I head to the room with the violinists where the wine fountain sits. As wine splashes into my glass, I hear someone behind me.

"Hi, Mom." I turn around to see Sienna. My heart melts.

I walk closer and gather her up in my embrace. Sienna relaxes as if she's putting down a weapon and slowly hugs me back.

EPILOGUE:

Sometimes things happen, and we don't know at the time what they mean. The way I process information, I've learned to trust it at that moment. I know that when I look back, it can have a different meaning than it did at first. It wasn't wrong then. In fact, it had been the truth then. But time and new information give the same occurrence new meaning. At first, I thought this was something incorrect in my thinking, but I've come to understand that what I see at first is real, even if hindsight changes my beliefs. Memory of the visitor when I was staying at the cabin on Lake Lure is one of those moments. She came one day while I was painting. She knocked on the door, I let her in, and a butterfly followed behind her. She introduced herself as Rose.

Rose told me a few stories that her family had passed down through generations. She used to live in the area, and the next-door neighbors back then used to be her friends. I didn't ask her how old she was, but I assumed she was in her sixties. I also didn't ask her why she came to my door instead of the neighbors'.

She spoke about the area and the history, how Rumbling Bald Mountain got its name. There was a time in the 1870s, before the lake had water. The preacher for a local church spoke of asking God to move the hearts of sinners by making the mountain shake beneath their feet. The next day, the mountain began to rumble intermittently. It continued for six months. The third oldest river in the world, the French Broad River, rippled with its rumbling.

Livestock had no place safe to run. It was pure chaos. People repented of their sins, thinking the world was ending.

I found it fascinating how the earth could speak to them so profoundly and for quite some time, as if giving them time to contemplate their life's purpose.

Rose lived in Cherokee, North Carolina. She was part Cherokee. I asked if there was a record of this occurrence. She told me how scientists later explained that it was likely rocks falling under the mountain in a hidden cave system. The preacher's premonition had no scientific explanation. I asked her how her family defined what had happened, her Cherokee elders. She didn't know, but we spent a couple of hours coming up with our own theories.

I think now about this phenomenon that occurred in a place where I resided for a month. I think how, as humans, we become so obsessed with ourselves and forget the environment and what's outside of us. The tunnel vision of our world and the depression that results from the lack of awareness of how we're connected to other people and our environment. It still happens, regardless of whether we know it or not, yet we struggle to tap into this understanding and capitalize on it, the connection.

I came up with my own theories about how Rumbling Bald got its name, trying to make sense of this world, things we won't ever know for sure, or maybe will learn about later. My environment was trying to heal me, and I let it. If you think about it, isn't the earth trying to heal and balance itself as well? There are truths that we can't possibly understand because our brains are incapable of knowing and absorbing them.

Countries, culture, define our construct—we can suffer from these constructs if we're on the wrong side. Many things we can't see, we can't know, at certain times, places, and positions within this construct. How do we deal with the lack of information? One could say we're always dealing with a lack of information. But we made this all up, so why do we suffer?

All these things are what we created as a human race. The constructs, the rules, money, what is valued and important. Why are we making such a big deal about it when it's inherent in us that we have the power to change it, since humans are the ones who created it in the first place? This knowledge and understanding gives me relief and makes me able to forget that it was several humans together who created the structure in which I live and influence the way I feel. How hard it is to grasp or remember that this is what's happening all the time. How can we fall into just believing and blindly follow? How can we get so lost in it all?

I found out later that Rose was the owner of the cabin. She came by for a chat and never let on she owned it. Rose was a guest in her own home and let me be the hostess. Looking back, I saw traces of her throughout the house.

She never mentioned anything peculiar about the cabin, or that it was haunted. Rose just felt it was important to come back and visit the place. She felt the rumbling back then meant the land was sacred and special. It was the earth speaking to us and telling us to be authentic in our pursuit of who we are, to listen to the whispering around us. We're so busy in our heads that we forget to listen to what's going on outside of us. She emphasized how we should not only connect with the earth, but with the people around us, no matter what. I have the perspective now to realize how true this is.

My mind had led me astray, but when I finally listened to the rhythm, it brought me back to where I needed to be.

Black Butterfly

ACKNOWLEDGMENTS:

First and foremost, thank you to the forces that aligned to allow a rare cabin trip to Lake Lure with my two daughters in early spring 2021. The novelty of being alone with my girls inspired my passion to write a novel. Thank you to the little mouse that decided to come out for a popcorn snack and scare the shit out of me. The short-lived mystery of *what could possibly be making that noise* sparked the initial idea of *Black Butterfly*. What resulted in the final story is a lot more difficult to explain.

Thank you to my friends, family, neighbors, and acquaintances for having interesting lives, experiences, and personalities that inspired the fictional characters in this story. I found my knack for character development there.

Thank you, Maya, for being incredibly kindhearted and my little promoter. Thank you, Francesca, for being an unwavering force of strength and disruptor of norms.

I've been a lifelong writer, but never a novelist. It's a whole other skillset that I didn't study in school. Thank you to the online masterclass platform and numerous authors who posted their classes on their expertise. These authors included: Judy Blume, James Patterson, Amy Tan, Margaret Atwood, Dan Brown, and Salmon Rushdie. Thank you to the leaders at the Atlanta Writers

Club for organizing workshops, meetings, speakers, and conferences that allow newbies to connect and learn about the industry.

To my editors and beta readers, I appreciate your guidance during my steep learning curve in writing my first novel: Janie Mills, Sharon Marchisello, Stacey Parshall Jensen, Cyndi Sandusky, and Tamian Wood. The story wouldn't land the same or be as strong without your suggestions and expertise.

Last, but not least, thank you to the enigmatic butterfly for being a symbolic representation and inspiration of hope, transformation, beauty, and magic.

ABOUT THE AUTHOR:

Claudia Jones is driven by an instinctive pull toward truth, mystery, and hidden threads that tie human experiences together. Through storytelling, she explores awakening, identity, and the quiet power that emerges from breaking old patterns.

When she isn't writing, she spends her time caring for her animals and connecting with her children. She believes in the transformative nature of love, timing, and creative expression. She recently moved to Chattanooga, Tennessee and she's enjoying a fresh start on top of a mountain.

www.ingramcontent.com/pod-product-compliance
Lightning Source LLC
LaVergne TN
LVHW091716070526
838199LV00050B/2417